BOOKS BY JEFFREY POSTON

ACTION/ADVENTURE THRILLERS

American Terrorist: Where is the Girl?
Contagion: American Terrorist 2
Escalate! American Terrorist 3
American Terrorist Trilogy

Joshua Experiment (Call Sign: Raven Book 1)
The End of Everything (Call Sign: Raven Book 2)
The Queen (Call Sign: Raven Book 3)

JASON PEARES HISTORICAL WESTERNS

Courage (Book 1)
Legacy of an Outlaw (Book 2)
Warriors (Book 3)
Manhunter (Book 4)

LEGACY OF AN OUTLAW (THE PEACEKEEPER)

"Poston's [Jason] Peares walks into trouble at every turn. He's tough, quick with a gun, and understanding of the underdog."

—Steven Havill, author of *Privileged to Kill*

"A fast-moving story of guns and gunfighters, with a climactic cattle stampede of Texas-caliber proportions."

—Elmer Kelton, author of *Cloudy in the West*

"An exciting, page-turning traditional western sure to please. Fine work."

—Norman Zollinger, author of *Rage in Chupadera*

"Poston's stylishly written action yarn will generate a strong following among western fans."

—Wes Lukowsky, American Library Association

COURAGE

"Jeffrey Poston understands the craft of constructing his novel and does a wonderful job balancing narrative elements with his dialogue. When his protagonist handles his firearms, you know the author has done his research in describing the action."

—Phillip Hardy, Lulu.com review

A MAN CALLED TROUBLE

"In his first novel, Jeffrey A. Poston has numbered himself among the best writers of westerns working today."

—Biblio.com review Praise for Jeffrey Poston

WARRIORS

"It doesn't get any more real than this."

—D. Brock, Silver City, NM

LEGACY of an OUTLAW

A Jason Peares Western

JEFFREY POSTON

LOMAS & TURNER PRESS

Ordering Information:

Quantity sales. Special discounts are available on quantity purchases by corporations, associations, and others. Orders by U.S. trade bookstores and wholesalers. For details, contact the publisher at the address above.

Editing by The Pro Book Editor
Cover design by Deanna Dionne
Interior design by IAPS.rocks

eBook ISBN: 978-0-9916194-3-6
paperback ISBN: 978-0-9863328-4-5

    1. Main category—Fiction/Westerns
    2. Other category—Fiction/Action and Adventure

First Edition

CHAPTER I

J AY WAS LOST. HIS PURSUERS had chased him into the canyons about a day's ride east of Gallup, New Mexico. Now he had nowhere left to go.

Red rock was everywhere, colored by nature thousands of years ago, tinted by the setting sun. And some of it was colored by the blood of Jay's hunters. The body of one of the men lay a hundred feet below Jay. Another dead body lay on the cliff top fifty feet above his head.

He looked around slowly, careful not to move too quickly in the growing shadows. Sudden movement would surely draw more gunfire. He situated his precarious balance in the narrow chimney, his right boot tip and both hands in front and his left boot heel in a small crevasse in the wall behind his back. Then he looked down.

Somewhere around the cliff, four more men waited or maneuvered to find him. If he could just make the ledge only twenty feet below, he might survive. That would mean climbing twenty feet straight down without slipping, without making noise, and without being seen.

Hoping he could find handholds and footholds.

In the dark.

Jay shook his head as he slowly sought another toehold for his right boot. If only he had minded his own business back in town the day before, he'd be riding the range right now, unbothered and most certainly un-hunted. But there was no way Jay could have stood by silently when he saw a couple of kids being harassed by grown men.

The boy looked to be about sixteen, the girl maybe a year older. The boy was White, the girl was Black. After rinsing the trail dust down with a couple of watered-down whiskeys in the saloon, Jay had seen the couple crossing the road a bit up from the saloon. Three men were blocking the pathway of the pair. Jay's horse was across the road, so he could have walked directly to his mount and avoided the squabble altogether. But he took the long route and ended up in the middle of the mess.

The boy had a gun stuck in his belt and the brown-skinned girl stood behind him. Facing the boy were three motley cowhands, fingers itching to draw and settle the issue.

"Let me see if I got this straight," Jay had said, interrupting the confrontation.

Jay had caught them off guard when he walked up behind the three men as they were picking a fight with the boy. "You're going to shoot this young man because he's tryin' to run off with someone's wife."

"That ain't true," the girl said quickly. "I ain't married to nobody!"

Jay's bright brown eyes drilled into those of the leader of the trio.

"But I thought you said that she was some Benton feller's lady."

He had placed himself between the three men and the couple. Around them, people who had been milling about seemed to sense the trouble brewing and scurried to safety. A quick glance in all directions informed Jay that no one was in the way of bullets if gunfire erupted.

"Now, listen here," one of the troublemakers said. "I didn't say she was married. I said she belonged to Mr.—"

"Oh, I see," Jay interrupted, nodding as if suddenly struck by the obvious. "You mean she's his slave."

The man started to speak, then stopped.

"I seem to recollect that slavery ended about ten years ago.

2

Or do you mean to tell me Mr. Benton is this girl's daddy?" Jay said mockingly.

"This is between them and us," the man who seemed to be the leader said quietly. Saliva dribbled from his lip and down into his beard as he spat tobacco juice. "Don't concern you."

"Yeah," said another. "We had enough of your smart talk. As far as I'm concerned, your kind is agreeable only one way and that's dead."

"And what kind would that be?"

The third troublemaker took a step forward and spoke up.

"Listen, you half-breed son of a—"

Jay's eyes flared, and his right arm moved in a blur. He brought his gun up, flipped it so he held it by the barrel, and slammed the gun butt upside the man's head. There was a dull thud, and the troublemaker's eyes rolled up in his head and closed before he flopped down in the dirt.

The two other men stood motionless for a split second, stunned. The leader lowered his hand toward his gun but stopped when he stared down the barrel of Jay's second gun. The other troublemaker had his gun halfway out but quickly opened his hand and let his gun fall back to rest.

Jay spoke quietly. "I reckon this is a good time to reconsider your position."

"This ain't finished," the man said as he eyed the young boy and his girl. Then he and his partner dragged the unconscious man to their horses. They threw the man over his saddle and mounted up. The leader took another long, glaring look at Jay, who followed their every movement with drawn guns. The men finally turned and rode out of town.

The girl spoke shakily. "Thanks, mister. I don't know who you are, but I'm mighty glad for your help."

"I guess I just hate to see anybody disrespectful of a lady." Jay tipped his hat and turned to the boy. "You sure you know what you're gettin' yourselves into?"

The young man nodded. "Mister, I can take care of myself. And her."

"I don't doubt it a bit. But I can't say you're takin' the easiest path to happiness. There'll be others like them. There always are."

"We love each other," the girl offered meekly. "We'll make it."

"That's right," the young man said defiantly.

"Well, even still, if I were you, I'd put a few days' distance between here and wherever." Jay turned to leave.

"Hey!"

Jay turned back.

"I'm obliged to you, mister," the young man said.

Jay waved and mounted his horse. He sat tall in the saddle. Thin, yet tightly muscular, he wore simple brown corduroy pants and a plaid cotton shirt. Short, slightly curly black hair hid beneath his hat and several days' stubble merged his narrow mustache with a sparse beard. His skin was very light brown.

As he rode out of town, he thought about the young couple. *Sure they were in love,* he reflected. *And the boy probably could protect his woman from all but the most determined troublemakers that came looking for them. But they'd find that kind of life relentlessly hard and dangerous.*

He wondered whether they had considered what life would be like for their children.

If they decided to make a family, their children would be half-White and half-Black, like Jay. If times didn't change, and they never did, their kids would probably grow up loners, shunned by Whites and Blacks, part of both races, yet part of neither. Like Jay. Stuck in the middle.

When he was barely old enough to ride a pony, Jay's parents had moved the family north, then west, from Kentucky to Missouri, trying to avoid persecution by those who were fervently opposed to a mixed marriage. Even after the war, his father, a proud Negro war veteran who had lost a leg in one of the final battles, began to talk about moving again as if he could outdistance the problem.

Jay shuddered at the uncomfortable memories of his childhood. Maybe someday he'd find a way to deal with those thoughts. For now, he turned his attention to the beauty of the open land along the trail.

The next day he noticed a dust trail following him in the distance. He guessed the troublemakers from town were in front of the pack since the leader had said it wasn't finished. The men pursuing him knew the red rock canyons intimately. That much was clear to Jay now. They had surrounded him, herding him up a dead-end box canyon to the edge of the cliff, where he'd had no choice except to dismount and try to flee into the rocks on foot.

Now, Jay looked down at the dead body far below him in the growing darkness. He had recognized the face of the leader from town as the man plummeted from above with Jay's bullet in his belly. The man had screamed all the way down. It was finished now, at least for him.

Jay climbed down to within reach of the ledge. He stretched his left leg around the corner of the ledge to gain a foothold, then carefully leaned out of the chimney. As he glanced down, he saw the ledge was barely eighteen inches wide. That was all that separated him from the grasp of death waiting on the canyon floor seventy feet below.

Above him, one of the hunters finally found the steep crevasse and peered down, shouting as he saw Jay moving out of sight. His gunshot echoed through the canyon, and the rock in Jay's right-hand grip exploded.

Thrown off-balance, Jay teetered backward. He fought the panicked urge to grab for the nearly smooth surface of the wall, knowing such movement would force him farther from it. Instead, he crouched to try to steady himself, but still he felt the inevitable tug of gravity pulling him away from the ledge. In desperation, Jay kicked both feet off the narrow ledge in a frantic effort to rotate his upper body back toward the wall. Then he dropped, flailing his arms at nothing, at anything.

As he fell, his chest scraped against the ledge. He caught hold, barely, and his chin banged hard on the rock. He tasted the sweet warmth of blood from a split tongue as he desperately clawed at the ledge.

For a moment, Jay entertained the brief thought that he was safe. Then shouts and echoes filled the air as footsteps came from his left. Someone else had found the ledge.

Jay tried to climb back onto the ledge, but there was no room to scramble up sideways. He moved hand-over-hand back toward the chimney, where he knew he could at least get a foothold, but another gunshot discouraged him quickly.

Jay looked around again for options, but there were few. He slid his feet around as much as he could, grappling for even the smallest crack or outcrop to grip, but the wall had been worn smooth by eons of wind and rain. There simply was nothing for him to take hold of.

All because of those kids, he thought, as he tried to work a kink out of his shoulder. No, it wasn't their fault he'd stuck his nose in their business. He could just as easily have avoided his friend and shadow, trouble, and ridden out of town—left the boy to die and the girl to a fate worse than death.

Not likely. He knew he would have found it hard to live with himself if he had. He had the tools and the skills—fast guns and reflexes—to help folks who couldn't help themselves. So he did.

Now he accepted the helplessness of his own situation and struggled to get both elbows up onto the ledge. Then he began to crawl slowly, carefully, toward an unseen escape route around the bend in the ledge. He was just about to peer around the bend when a boot suddenly appeared right next to him.

Craning his neck, Jay looked up into a face with a sinister grin, a face that saw victory. The man's hand that gripped the wall disappeared for a moment, then reappeared seconds later holding a gun.

There was nothing Jay could do except lash out. He grabbed the man's boot and pulled it toward him with all the strength he could muster, then clawed at the ledge again as he began to slip. Jay heard a gasp as the man fell past him. The gunman reached out as he fell, grabbing Jay's left boot. As Jay began to slip again, his boot slid out of the man's grasp and the man fell, screaming all the way to the canyon floor.

Breathing a sigh of relief, Jay clutched his way hand-over-hand to a wide section around the bend of the ledge. Despite his slippery, bleeding hands and elbows, he managed to crawl up onto the ledge. He lay there for a moment, trying to catch his breath and calm his nerves.

When he finally collected his wits and got to his feet, he looked up to find a steep path where a massive split in the cliff wall had opened up a long time ago. It formed a narrow rift Jay followed back to the top of the plateau.

Somewhere nearby, there were still three men after him. They would surely kill him if he did not kill them first unless he could find his way back to the horses and escape without more killing.

Jay was lost. Most of the canyon and the entire rift in the cliff were in deep shadow. Jay thought he was safe, but when he heard the sound above him, he realized his mistake.

Someone perched on the plateau above waited for him on the edge. Jay looked up as the man's gun cleared its leather holster.

Jay spun against the rock wall and drew both guns as shots blasted from above and sent whining ricochets into the darkness. Chunks of rock exploded around him. He fired back, aiming wildly at the brief flash of light from the man's gun barrel. A scream of pain echoed from above, and the man fell right at Jay's feet.

The man's gunshot injury was only a minor flesh wound, but the fall had left him unconscious. He kicked the man's gun over the ledge while he holstered his own guns. As he scrambled up the incline, Jay heard more running footsteps approaching. He raced out of the rift, rounded a huge boulder just ahead of the gunfire, and ran right into the ground-tied horses. Without breaking his stride, Jay jumped into the saddle of his own horse. With a shout and a kick from a single boot spur, he raced away, dragging two of the men's mounts with him. Shouts and wild gunshots followed him, but he was clear. He knew that particular scrape had been closer than most. He didn't know where the rest of his pursuers' horses were, but he led the two animals far enough away so the survivors wouldn't find them.

He rode through the night. Dawn found him in the north-western part of New Mexico, near the town of Gallup. He had just topped a small rise when he heard a noise close by, back to his right. He instinctively reached for a gun, but a voice from behind froze him.

"I wouldn't do that, sir."

Jay slowly turned in his saddle to face a reed-thin, beady-eyed man who looked like he hadn't shaved in a whole month. The man seemed to have appeared magically from behind a tall cactus. His rifle was aimed in the center of Jay's chest.

"You lookin' for trouble, mister?" the man asked, glaring at Jay.

He wore a low, narrow-brimmed hat, and his long, unkempt black hair reached to his shoulders. His black handlebar mustache and beard combined to give him a downright sinister look.

"I'm lookin' to avoid it," Jay answered, nodding back over his right shoulder. Riders rounded the hill and pulled up hard.

"Those are my boys. Huntin' rustlers. Now, I don't suppose you seen any?"

Jay caught the accusation in the man's voice. "Whatever trouble is brewing hereabouts is none of my concern."

"Well, if you ain't stealin' my cows, what the hell are you doin' in these parts?"

"Had me a run-in with some disagreeable fellas yesterday who decided to follow me into the canyon over yonder," Jay said. "Lost a boot in the process," he added, trying to ease the tension.

Jay looked around cautiously at his diminishing escape options as the seven riders rode slowly up the hill toward him. He turned his horse sideways, his left side toward the riders and his right toward the man with the rifle. His hands hovered over his gun butts.

"Hold on now," the man said, waving a hand in a subduing gesture toward the riders. "I don't think this here's the one we're looking for. He ain't even got no rope."

"Yeah," agreed one of the newcomers. "Can't change a cattle brand without a rope."

Another added, "I ain't never seen no rustlers without boots." The man could only see Jay's stocking-clad left foot. "Too many damned stickers all over the place."

"He don't look like the rustlin' type," returned the first. "Looks more like a gunfighter. No offense to you, mister."

"Nonc takcn," Jay answered.

The man on the ground lowered his rifle and took a few steps toward Jay. "You know anything about cows?"

Jay nodded uneasily. "I've run a few over the years."

"Well, my name's Cassie." The man extended a bony hand. "We ain't 'bout nothin' but an honest day's work."

"I'm Jay." Jay returned the handshake.

"I sure could use another hand," Cassie said. "Can't pay much, only three dollars a month...and that's only if we get them critters back over to Texas, to their rightful owner. Then we'll pick up a fresh herd and run 'em up north."

Jay was introduced, and the group rode around the hill and down into camp. A large herd of cattle grazed peacefully in the valley beyond the camp. He could smell the breakfast long before he saw the elderly cook piling food onto dented metal plates. Suddenly, his stomach set to growling fiercely.

Stuffing his face with grub and watching the group interact, Jay regretted prejudging Cassie and his men. They looked to be a hard bunch, rough around the edges a bit, but they seemed to be nothing more than hard workers—real people trying to carve an honest life out of the rugged countryside. Three of the men looked like brothers, and the rest acted like longtime friends.

Kinfolk and friends. Relationships Jay hadn't known for longer than he could remember.

Another cattle run wouldn't hurt. After all, it was something to do for a while, and Jay certainly didn't mind having people around that he didn't have to worry about turning his back on. And his wages would replace the money he'd have to spend on a new pair of boots.

CHAPTER 2

FOUR DAYS PASSED BEFORE JAY found some used boots to trade for at a passing wagon train. The trade cost him a gun and a box of shells, but he had spares of both in his saddle pack.

The cattle drive lasted far longer than it should have, mostly on account of an inexperienced ramrod and crew. But they lost only a small number of animals, and education came quick for the newcomers to the business of running cattle. They finally got their livestock back to Texas and ran a new herd up to Wyoming. The return trip ended deep down near the Gulf Coast, in a port town Jay never even bothered to learn the name of.

The town bristled with all manner of activity, but Jay didn't hang around long enough to see much of it. There were too many people, and there was always the chance that someone would recognize him. Instead, Jay took his meager thirteen dollars and said his farewells. Then he was back in the saddle again.

For a while, he was glad to be out in the open again. Soon he was weary of having nowhere in particular to go.

It was the beginning of May. Spring's handiwork was all about. Not that there was much to see or look at, but at least all the scrub grass was green, and the dandelion weeds had pretty yellow flowers waving in the wind. From the top of the low hill, Jay could see the entire countryside in all directions. To the north lay nothing but scrub grass. To the northwest, he saw a town about six or seven miles away, and to the west and southwest more hills rolled into the distance. Behind him to the south and east lay mile after mile of empty plains.

Two months in the saddle and he was still in Texas. He was beginning to think the whole United States was just a small corner of a big Texas! Last week, he had ridden for two whole days without even seeing a tree. Today, all he wanted was a hot bath, a hot meal, and a soft bed to sleep on, and it was all only six miles away. After that, he would simply pass on.

Pass on.

It seemed drifting was all he did nowadays. Mile after mile and year after year of endless cattle trails, at best making around five dollars a month when he was working, but sometimes bringing in ten if he rode with one of the big, well-organized crews. He chuckled at the thought of all the crazy folks back East who wanted to come out West for the adventure. Most of the time, life was lonely and boring. And when it wasn't boring, it was damned hard work.

He was tired of passing on. Four years of drifting through towns and states with no place to go and no reason to get there. With a suddenness born of boredom and recklessness, he decided right there in the saddle that California sounded like a pretty good destination. At least he was headed in the right direction.

Folks said California was just as big as Texas, if not bigger. No matter. A couple more weeks and he'd be across the northwest border of Texas and back into New Mexico. Maybe a few more weeks of empty land after that, where it was not likely anyone would find him.

California, it was said, possessed lots of unclaimed land. Maybe he could find peace and quiet and grow old out there, without having to keep looking over his shoulder. Maybe he could live a normal life.

Jay was so involved in his thoughts he almost didn't notice the woman off to his right, walking toward the town. He looked around again and wondered where she was walking from. The nearest hill was over three miles away. A minute later, he slowed his mount to walk beside her.

"Mornin', ma'am," Jay said, tipping his hat. The woman looked up at him warily, then nodded. "May I offer you a ride?"

"You may not."

They stared at each other. She was tall and slender, medium brown in complexion, with graying hair and a fair share of age lines around her eyes. Her short, curly hair was visible underneath a frazzled straw hat. Her ankle-length dress was made of plain muslin, tattered and worn thin. Well-worn rawhide sandals adorned her feet, and Jay could see a few of the desert goat-head stickers attached to her callused feet.

"My appearance bothers you," she said finally, watching him study her.

She gazed at Jay through green eyes that seemed to peer into his very soul. She stood tall and proud, her expression one of defiance.

"No, ma'am. But it bothers me to see you walking so far. I—"

"I'm not helpless, young man."

"I have no doubts about that, ma'am. But my ma, God rest her soul, would beat me from here to Mexico if I passed by without even offering you a ride."

Jay smiled and the woman smiled back, then extended her hand. Jay moved his right foot from the stirrup and scooted back to sit partly on his saddle pack, then helped the woman sideways up into the saddle.

She turned to thank Jay but stopped, only staring at him with an empty gaze, like she was considering some distant memory. After a few seconds, the smile returned, and she patted Jay's hand. He kicked the horse into a slow walk.

"Why, you're a Colored boy, aren't you?"

"I had mixed parents, ma'am."

She looked at him again, her eyes drifting down toward his double-gun holster. She nodded knowingly.

"I'm Winifred Evans," she said.

"I'm Jay."

"Jay what?"

"Just Jay."

"Well, no, that's not entirely true, is it?"

A warning tingled up his spine, but his clear brown eyes showed no emotion.

"And what makes you think that, Miss Evans?"

She looked deep into his eyes, then patted his hand again and smiled knowingly. Then she turned to face forward, her mind apparently on other things.

Jay frowned. The woman couldn't possibly know him, but maybe she knew of him. Maybe she'd somehow heard that the outlaw gunfighter was traveling through Texas, and she recognized him from a description. Wouldn't be too many gunfighters that looked like him in these parts. He had to be extra careful, never let his diligence falter. There was no way to be sure, but as always, Jay would turn his back on no one. He set those thoughts aside as he turned up the main street of the town.

The town had one other street parallel to the main street and two side streets crossing the town from north to south. Winifred Evans pointed to the church at the west end of town, and Jay rode up the street. He glanced casually from side to side while the woman watched him, and his left hand was never far from his holster.

Just in case.

Jay noticed the woman studying him, and it made him a bit uneasy. His was the caution and habit born from years of being hunted and surviving—an outlaw's life. Even though he was no longer wanted by the law, he had killed a few bounty hunters since his acquittal. There were still angry kinfolk somewhere wanting revenge. Some had found him and more often than not, they'd found him in small, innocent-looking towns like this one.

Jay realized it was Sunday, church day, as he watched people filter into the small white church building. He stopped and helped the woman down, politely refusing her invitation to join her. As he reined around to leave, she called to him.

"You be careful, Jason. Trouble is not far away."

She turned and disappeared through the church doorway, leaving Jay sitting stunned in his saddle. *Why would she say that? And she called me Jason! How could she possibly know?* He shook his head. He hadn't used his real name—Jason Peares— in years. *She must have assumed Jay was short for Jason, her warning merely a friendly caution,* he thought as he turned to make his way back up the street. Or perhaps there was a rumor about his whereabouts, as impossible as that seemed.

As he rode, he heard a whisper and glanced at a Black family of four moving their buckboard to park across the street from the church. The whisper came from a young lady chastising a boy about four years old not to point at "the brown-skinned stranger wearing the guns."

The young woman was more than pretty, Jay noticed, and she smiled in his direction. Jay tipped his hat and eyed her for a long moment, then heard an older man, probably her father, clearing his throat and glaring at him. Jay nodded respectfully, turned away, and continued riding up the street.

Jay passed several stores of food and supplies and farm equipment before riding up to the only boardinghouse in town. The sign claimed "Rooms For Rent," and Jay assumed that a bathtub could be found inside. He dismounted and tied his horse to the hitching rail, then took one last glance around before going inside. He noticed a short, overweight man in a loose-fitting white suit and matching hat walking out of the saloon two shops up the street. He was followed by a huge bald companion, and both men were looking his way.

Jay watched them as he closed the door behind him, but they made no move toward him. They might be trouble or they might not, but Jay was ready as always. He walked to the reception desk where an elderly man with thinning white hair sat reading a newspaper through thick wire-rimmed lenses.

"Excuse me, can I have a bath and shave?" Jay asked quietly.

The old man didn't move or even look up, just kept reading his paper. Jay spoke a little louder.

"Excuse me, can I have a bath and shave?"

This time the old man heard him and stood to face Jay.

"Sorry, young man," he croaked. "Didn't see you come in. What can I do for you?"

"I'd like a bath and shave, please."

"You'll have to speak up a bit." He leaned forward, favoring his right ear. "I can't hear like I used to when I was your age."

"I'd like a bath and shave, please," Jay shouted.

"Well, I can fix you up some bath water, but you'll have to go down the street for a shave."

The old man led the way into a side room and Jay watched him hunt through several cabinet drawers. Finally, he located a stiff-bristle brush and a greasy bar of soap that he tossed into the huge tub already half-full with water.

Jay found the tub interesting. He hadn't seen one quite like it before and wondered if the old man had built it himself. It sat on a sturdy wood stand under which lay a short squat stove. The stove could be fired up to quickly heat the water and the heavy cast-iron stove would keep the water warm for some time. The tub even had a drain hole punched in the bottom that let the water pour out through a roughly cut, square hole in the floor to soak into the dirt under the hotel. A ragged wooden cork plugged the drain hole.

Jay leaned against the wall, yawning, while the old man fumbled to strike up a fire in the stove. The man moved too slowly for his liking, so Jay decided to help out or he'd be there all day. He rapped a knuckle on the stove's exhaust pipe to get the man's attention.

"Here, let me do it."

The old man handed Jay the matches and a bucket of kindling and scuttled out of the room. Jay closed the door behind him and locked it. He set one gun on each side of the tub—in case someone tried to surprise him—and stripped. Then, he settled on the side of the tub, waiting for the water to get warm.

Two hours later, he emerged into the sunlight feeling like a new man. He had washed off two months of dirt and grit and was now ready for a shave. He walked down the street to the barber's, again noticing the man in white and his companion watching from the saloon doorway.

Jay turned and stared up the street at the two men, letting them know he knew they were there. The short man smiled friendly-like and waved, but the big, bald man just stood there at his side. Jay ignored the greeting and simply turned away to step into the barbershop. He looked at the single empty chair and the man standing behind it.

"Can I get a shave?"

"Sho'nuff. Just take them pea-shooters off an' have a seat." The man was all smiles behind his dirty white apron and passed a big beefy hand through shoulder-length brown hair.

Jay unbuckled his gun belt, hung his guns and hat on the rack, and walked over to the chair.

After he sat down, the barber took out an abnormally long razor and said, "Besides, it's been awhile since I shaved me a Negro." He played the razor across a sharpening stone. "An' I hear y'all's skin is thicker than ours too," he said with a grin. "I guess I better use my big blade, eh?"

Jay reached under his right pants leg and pulled out the hunting knife he kept hidden in a leg sheath. It was light bluish-gray in tint and was a one-piece knife carved from the bone of a buffalo—a gift from a grateful Indian friend years before. He laid the ten-inch knife in his lap, then took a long and comfortable breath and leaned far back in the reclined chair. He stared up menacingly at the barber.

"Use whatever blade you want. Just be sure you don't slip," Jay said, patting his own knife blade against the palm of his left hand. His knife was easily twice as long as the razor.

"Uh, on second thought, maybe I oughta use my regular blade?"

"Maybe you oughta." Jay smiled and closed his eyes as the barber replaced the razor with a more reasonable one and went to work.

A half hour later, Jay paid the man and strolled back up and across the street, heading for the kitchen. Inside, he ordered an extra-large steak with all the fixings. Then he sat in a front corner where he could see the entire room and look out the front windows. Fifteen minutes later, he was enjoying a huge juicy steak that covered his entire plate. A basket on the side was piled high with buttered biscuits. He took one and dunked it in his steaming black coffee, then savored the first bite.

As he was swallowing his second bite of the medium-rare meat, the man in the white suit and his huge companion walked into the kitchen and headed for his table. Jay noticed the man was not overweight, as he had previously thought from up the street. The man was short, and he was powerfully built with a barrel chest and thick muscles under his too-large suit. Jay estimated his age to be somewhere between forty and fifty. He had short gray-white hair, mustache, and beard. His angular face seemed a bit too small for his head, which seemed to bypass his neck and connect directly to his massive shoulders. Under his white suit jacket, the man wore a white shirt topped by a black bolo tie with a clasp adorned by large turquoise stones. In his right hand, he carried his white hat, and in his left, he gripped a crumpled white kerchief.

Dark stabbing eyes highlighted the man's sharp facial bone structure. Jay knew immediately this was not a man to trifle with.

As the two men approached his table, Jay pulled one of his guns from his holster and laid it in plain view on the table. It was a clear warning. The man seemed not to mind, though. He just smiled and extended his hand.

"Welcome to Bronco. My name's Pritchett, and this is Bull," he said, nodding to his companion. "And you are?"

"Hungry, if you don't mind."

Jay stuffed another biscuit in his mouth and ignored the intruders. There was something about the man he didn't like. He was too friendly in unfriendly territory. But he didn't look like the friendly sort. He wanted something.

"That's okay," Pritchett said. "I'll talk, you listen."

Pritchett pulled aside a chair and started to sit. As he squatted, Jay deftly palmed the gun from the table and pointed the barrel between Pritchett's eyes, barely an inch from his head.

"Perhaps you didn't quite understand me," Jay mumbled through a mouthful of food.

Pritchett simply straightened up and raised his hands in mock surrender, then turned for the door. Jay put the gun down and started for his fork again, only catching a glimpse of movement beside him. Without warning, Pritchett's bodyguard grabbed Jay's right hand. Bull was as fast and agile as a cat. Jay didn't even have time to flinch as the man's steel grip yanked him out of his chair and tossed him effortlessly through the air.

Jay tumbled as he crashed to the floor and pulled his left gun as Bull lunged toward him. Even as he cocked the hammer and swung to aim, he knew Bull was too fast. A large hand swatted the gun aside with a jolt that sent pain ripping through Jay's shoulder. Then a huge fist struck the side of his head, hammering him backward into a wall. He heard laughs and jeers all around as folks stopped eating and gathered around to watch.

The onslaught stopped and for a moment, he felt as if the room were spinning around his head. He caught his breath as he rolled to his hands and knees; he saw Pritchett squatting beside him.

"Ready to listen yet?" Pritchett asked with a sneer.

Jay looked at the man, then around at the laughing faces and up at Bull. The man stood four feet away with his hands on his hips, his face showing no expression of anger or excitement. Jay had the impression of a dumb watchdog that barked—or in this case, punched—on command. Jay looked back at Pritchett.

"Not just yet," he said.

With that, Jay launched himself from a crouch, springing feet first into the big man's chest. The force of Jay's 180 pounds drove the man back into a support pillar. The big man bounced forward with fire in his eyes.

Jay slammed a spinning sidekick to the man's midsection, then landed a forward jump-kick to his face when the man refused to yield. As blood splattered from Bull's face, Jay realized all he'd done was make him mad. Bull charged, and Jay dropped to the floor and spin-kicked, his left leg knocking Bull's feet out from under him. The wood floor creaked as the man crashed to the floor.

With a roar, he was back on his feet, advancing and swinging his colossal fists. Jay backpedaled, moving his arms up to deflect the big man's blows. Then came a swing that was wild and high, and Jay stepped in close.

Jay caught the fist and rotated it down and to the right, pulling Bull down over him. In the same motion, Jay ducked and swung the man onto his back, then bucked his butt high and flipped the big man straight through the front window and onto the boardwalk outside.

The wood creaked under the impact, and a shower of glass shards rained down on the man as he groaned and rolled slowly to his knees, dazed. Then, he shakily got to his feet and started back through the window, but Pritchett motioned him to stay outside.

Jay turned to Pritchett, brushing debris from his clothes. "Now we can talk," Jay said as he retrieved his guns. "After you buy me another steak."

Pritchett smiled, reached into his pant pocket, and flipped a coin toward Jay. He shook his head in amazement, then turned and left the kitchen house.

The next steak was served and devoured without event and Jay left, pausing before crossing the street toward his horse.

He glanced around. There was no sight of Pritchett and Bull. Two young boys stopped cleaning up the glass from the boardwalk as Jay regarded them without much interest. He turned and strolled toward the church, his mind on a strange coincidence and the woman who had predicted it. The woman who seemed to know him and of his frequent encounters with the phenomenon he referred to as his friend and shadow—trouble.

Jay stopped a few feet to the side of the church's only door and waited patiently for another hour. He leaned against the church with his left knee bent a bit, boot heel resting comfortably against the wall. His hat was pulled forward over his eyes to shade against the high sun and to discourage a curious pass-erby from attempting conversation. He waited, deep in thought. Footsteps approached and a voice intruded, as if drawn to his reclusive attitude instead of deterred.

"You waitin' for someone, mister?"

Jay tilted his head up and gazed at a sheriff's badge on the vest of an unkempt, lanky blond man. The man stood with his feet wide apart and his thumbs hooked into his belt loops. His chest was puffed out as if demanding respect, and Jay sensed all that was weak about the man who hid behind the lawman's badge. The sheriff was probably one of Pritchett's lackeys, though Jay wasn't sure why that thought tumbled through his brain.

"I asked you a question," the man said as Jay studied him. "Are you waiting for someone?"

"I am." Jay's penetrating gaze burned into the sheriff's eyes.

"Well?" the sheriff said.

Jay figured the sheriff was not accustomed to defiance. Pritchett's power was undisputed and defying his sheriff was as bad as defying Pritchett himself. Jay had done exactly that.

Jay glared at the man for a few seconds more until the church door swung outward and people began to file out. He simply pushed himself away from the wall and started toward the door. The sheriff grabbed his arm. At the same time, the Black family Jay had seen earlier stepped through the door, their eyes instantly drawn toward the commotion. They saw the confrontation and stopped.

"I'm talking to you, boy!" The sheriff tightened his grip and pulled. Or tried to.

Jay hooked his free thumb around the sheriff's baby finger and broke the man's grip by twisting the finger away from his body. The sheriff gasped and stumbled forward to lessen the pain. Jay pulled the finger farther forward and propelled the man straight into the church wall, face first. The man bounced off hard and crumpled to the dirt. Jay knelt down beside him and spoke quietly.

"I'm not your boy, Sheriff, and I'm not bothering anybody. So go mind your own business."

He pulled the man's holstered gun and dumped the shells from the chamber, then tossed it several feet behind the man. There were too many people standing around who might get hurt if the sheriff decided to do something stupid to avenge his wounded pride.

Jay straightened and turned back toward the line of exiting churchgoers. He caught the young lady's eye again, then looked at her father. His expression openly asked the man for permission to speak with his daughter.

The father's expression softened a bit, and he nodded. Jay was just about to speak to the young lady when Winifred Evans stepped past the family and stole his attention. As the family left for their wagon, the elderly woman stepped close and gently touched the side of Jay's face, noting the large bruise.

"You've been hurt," she said simply.

He stared at her for a moment. She reached for his arm, and he escorted her back up the street toward his horse.

"You warned me when we met," he said. "How did you know?"

"I know many things."

"You know my real name. I want to know how."

Jay stopped walking and stared at her. She patted his arm and spoke.

"You can trust me, Jason," she said quietly, prompting him to keep walking. "I'm not your enemy."

Jay just grunted, but he continued walking with her.

"What kind of things do you know…about me?"

"I know a lot about many things."

CHAPTER 3

"**W**HAT'RE YOU TRYING TO DO? Get yourself killed?" Pritchett whacked the sheriff across the head with his hat.

"I had him, Mr. Pritchett!" spat out the sheriff, cowering from another hit. "If he hadn't damn near broke my finger—"

"He'd probably have put a bullet in your head. Go get those two kids out of jail and send them to me. I've got an idea."

The sheriff nodded and left.

Pritchett looked up at Bull. "If this new man passes my next test, I'll hire him." He paused. "You really should wash that blood off your face. It embarrasses me for people to see that my bodyguard got whipped. By one man."

Jay and Miss Evans passed the kitchen house silently as she regarded the destroyed window and its frame.

"You did that?"

"Not directly, fortunately," Jay answered with a half-smile. "But I caused it."

"You're a man of many talents, aren't you?"

"I can take care of myself, if that's what you mean."

"I know you can. Just as I know things about you or your background, I've also sensed your involvement with the young lady you saw at the church."

Jay chuckled and shook his head.

"I've already decided this town is too hot for me. I'm not getting involved with anybody here, Miss Evans. I'm not even hanging around this town. I'm leaving Bronco, headed for California, as soon as I see you home safe."

"I can take care of myself too. I'm not the reason you're gonna stay." She patted his arm knowingly.

Jay just smiled and let the woman enjoy her fantasies of what she thought she might know.

They started across the street toward where Jay had left his horse tied up. They were in the middle of the street when a hostile voice called out behind them.

"Hey! Why don't you take old Witch Lady home where she belongs?"

Jay turned to face two young men. The one in front, who seemed to be the leader, barely seemed old enough to use a razor. Jay looked him over and turned his back on them, figuring they were just a couple of rowdies looking for trouble. He led Miss Evans to the horse and helped her up into the saddle as he listened to a stream of obscenities from the young men.

Jay spoke to them with barely a turn of his head. "If you boys want some action, you better get away from here and look somewhere else."

"Yeah?" one said, his right palm stroking the worn handle of his six-gun. "I got some action right here in my holster. What are you gonna do about it?"

"For now, I'll just ignore you. But I have to advise you, if you pull those guns, I'm gonna kill you."

"We don't need no advice from no half-breed." The two young men laughed.

Jay spun, and all laughter stopped instantly. The boy on the right stared at the gun that had appeared in Jay's right hand as if by magic. He had to notice that Jay's gun barrel was pointed straight between his eyes.

"I don't like that word, kid. I've never liked that word. So my question to you is, what are you going to do?" Jay spoke quietly.

The young man glanced nervously at his partner and licked his lip.

"Apologize," he stammered. "I'm gonna apologize, mister."

Jay stared at the young man for a moment longer, then narrowed his eyes.

"Apology not accepted."

In one smooth motion, Jay straightened his right arm and cocked his gun.

"Jason, no!" Miss Evans shouted at him. "Don't kill him!"

She jumped down from the horse and clutched his arm, forcing him to lower his aim. The young man dropped to his knees in the dirt and pleaded silently with his eyes for Jay to spare his life.

Miss Evans spoke quietly. "That boy is not your enemy. He's just a pawn of others."

"Like *you* know who my enemies are now?"

She said nothing, just kind of pulled at him, suggesting they get back on the horse and leave.

Jay tucked his gun away with a glance at Miss Evans. "I just wanted to scare him a bit."

"I think you succeeded."

The young man slowly got to his feet. Jay looked at both of them.

"You boys have something else to say?" They shook their heads fiercely. "Then get the hell away from here."

The boys flinched as Jay waved them away, then they turned and ran. As Jay was about to help Miss Evans up onto the horse again, Pritchett and four other men stepped out of the saloon and walked toward him.

"That was some fast action if I ever saw any," Pritchett said. Jay realized that Pritchett and his men had watched the whole incident. "You need a job, son?"

"I ain't your son, and I'm just passing through."

Jay helped Miss Evans into the saddle.

"Where to?"

"I don't see how that concerns you."

"Hold on now." Pritchett held out his arms in appeasement. "I admit we got off on the wrong foot, Jason, but let me make amends. I'll pay fifty dollars a week."

Jay removed his foot from the stirrup. "My name's Jay, not Jason."

"All right, *Jay*," Pritchett said. "How about fifty dollars a week?"

"That's gunman's wages. Mine's not for hire."

"Not your guns, Jay. I need your brains. I need a man who won't shoot to kill when only a warning will do. What do you think?"

Jay said nothing as he stared at the short man. Finally, he said, "I think you're trying to sweet-talk me. What is it you *really* want?"

"All right, all right," Pritchett conceded, waving his hands in the air. "There's some squatters settling on my land, and I want them run off. And I got legal papers that give me the right to do so. But all I got is hotheaded gun-toters ready to shoot anybody that breathes too deep. I need a man with gun skills and thinking skills, like you. What do you say?"

Jay regarded Miss Evans for a moment, and she smiled, apparently knowing all along he would stay in town. He smiled back at her. After all, it was something to do for a while.

"All right, I'll hire on. Just so long as you understand I'm not hired to kill people. I'm nobody's gunfighter."

"Good. Then you can start surveying land tomorrow, Jay."

Pritchett turned to the big man at his side. "You've already met Bull, my bodyguard."

Jay regarded the big man. He stood at least seven feet tall and probably weighed more than 300 pounds of solid muscle with a little extra in the paunch.

"I tell ya," Pritchett continued. "I've seen Bull take on a dozen men at one time and never even get taken down once. Until you came along."

"I reckon I got lucky," Jay lied, then added truthfully, "But he ain't hurt near as much as me." Jay rubbed the side of his face and said to Bull, "No hard feelings?"

Bull nodded.

As Jay shook Bull's hand, he squinted as bright sunlight reflected off a large silver medallion outside the man's shirt. The shiny medallion hung from an ornately linked silver chain and was round with three diamond-shaped holes cut in its center.

"And that over yonder is my number two man, Chuck Peters. He'll lead the team that does the surveying."

Pritchett pointed to a tall, freckle-faced man with dirty red hair leaning against the doorway of the general store next door to the hotel. Peters nodded and Jay nodded in return, but so far he didn't like the looks of this bunch. Jay admitted that looks could be deceiving. After all, Cassie's hard-looking crew had turned out to be all right.

Pritchett pointed out his two "enforcers" standing next to Peters. Eddie Platt was a tall stick of a man who looked like he lived only for the next gunfight. He had a stringy mop of shoulder-length black hair over a black vest, black shirt, and black pants—obviously for their sinister look—and wore a low-slung double-gun holster. He acknowledged Jay with only a mean glare.

Jay knew Platt saw him only as a challenge. The gunfighter was itching for the contest. Jay was not impressed. All gunfighters knew the importance of keeping the tools of their trade clean, but Platt's guns looked like they hadn't been cleaned for a month.

The other man was Slade. Jay got the impression that he was by far the most dangerous of the bunch. The man's sky-blue eyes seemed to soak up every detail about Jay. But Slade's steady gaze carried neither threat nor intimidation. His hair was neatly cut, and he was clean-shaven and serious looking. His clothes were typical range wear, and his single left-handed holster was strapped over almost new riding leathers. He waved friendly-like as they were introduced, and Jay returned the greeting. But he knew this man was not a man to underestimate.

"And you can get a room right here in my hotel, where you got your bath." Pritchett pointed his thumb over his shoulder. He added with the glint of a smile in his eyes, "I knew you were the man for the job as soon as I saw you."

Pritchett's confidence disturbed Jay. His squat frame stood barely five and a half feet high, but he could easily tip a grain scale at 200 pounds.

"Yes, indeed. And you passed my test just fine so—"

"Test!" Jay said angrily. He took a menacing step toward Pritchett, then stopped and collected himself. He was badly outnumbered.

"I could've killed those boys." He backstepped and prepared to mount up. "Don't make that mistake again, Mr. Pritchett. Or maybe I'll see how you like to be tested."

"If you want to do some testing," Eddie Platt said as he walked over from the other men, "you'll have to come and talk to me first."

The man stopped a few feet from Pritchett and faced Jay, flexing his gun hand.

"I'll keep that in mind," Jay said, pulling himself onto his horse.

"Well, then," said Pritchett. "See you bright and early in the morning?"

"Sure."

"One more thing, Jay. I have only one simple rule. Give me my money's worth in work and don't cross me, or you'll have to answer directly to me." Pritchett shrugged.

"I have one simple rule, also," Jay said, staring down at Pritchett. "Any of your men bother Miss Evans here, and I shoot to kill."

Pritchett stared at Jay for a moment longer, then let out a gut-wrenching laugh. He pointed at Jay and laughed some more, slapping his side with his hat.

"That's good! You know, I like you, Jay. I really, really do. You're a man I can respect." He laughed again for a moment, then continued. "Hell, everybody else around here is afraid to even look at me sideways, but not you. No, you tell a man just what's on your mind."

Pritchett stepped closer to Jay's horse and then reached up for a handshake.

"I'll abide by your rule if you'll abide by mine."

"Fair enough," Jay said, leaning down to return the shake. "See you tomorrow morning."

Pritchett watched Jay ride off, looking after him until the gunfighter reached the east end of town and turned toward the southeast. Then he turned to his men.

"Well, what do you think?" he said to no one in particular. "A maverick, I'd say."

"He's all bluster. He backed down too easy," Platt said with contempt.

Behind him, Slade chuckled.

Platt turned to him and said, "What're you laughing at?"

"Platt, you don't know the difference between a man backing down because he's scared or because he doesn't want to have to kill you."

Eddie Platt glared at the gunfighter. Peters took his cue and quickly moved out of the way.

"You think you can take me, don't you?" Platt said to Slade.

"The possibility's there," Slade said, taunting him. "Of course, you might get lucky."

"Stand up and—"

"Now, now, boys," Pritchett stepped between them and guided them toward the saloon with a gentle hand. "Let's go get a drink."

Slade stood leaning against the general store wall for a second longer before he smiled at Pritchett and went along. After a few seconds, Pritchett dismissed Platt with a wave of his hand and addressed Slade.

"What do you think? You scared of that Jay fella?"

Slade chuckled. "You know better than to even ask that kind of question. A man doesn't earn a living very long in my line of work by being scared. Probably a good thing he's on our side, though."

"I had pretty much the same thought," Pritchett admitted as they passed through the swinging double doors of the saloon. "He's a bit like you, you know. Won't be pushed."

"Might be good to keep that in mind, Mr. Pritchett."

Pritchett stopped against the bar and looked at Slade, trying to determine how to interpret the man.

"Relax, Mr. Pritchett," Slade continued. "You and me, we aren't friends by far, but as long as your money's good, so is my service."

"Agreed."

Half a mile out beyond the town, Jay wrestled with his impressions of Pritchett's group. Slade was not only dangerous, but there had been a hint of wary recognition in the man's eyes. Maybe Slade had not been able to place him completely, didn't know his real name, but he seemed to respond to Jay with a distant familiarity, like the kindred spirit that gunfighters share.

As sure as the sun rose in the east, Slade would be a deadly opponent if crossed. Jay shook the thoughts from his mind and turned his attention to Miss Evans in the saddle in front of him.

"The Witch Lady, eh?" Jay said after a while.

"I've been called worse things, mostly by people who don't understand my abilities. But you understand, don't you?"

Jay sensed her vulnerability. "I've heard of your kind. You've got a special gift."

People with the gift could glimpse pieces of the future or the past or seemed to know things about people they had never met. They were feared and hated, cast out to live alone unless they learned to hide their ability.

"Just how much do you know about me?"

"Not very much."

Jay chuckled at her evasion. "How exactly do you know things about me?"

"Every time I touch you, I learn something more about you. Some people are special, connected in some spiritual way. But most people never know it. I can touch that spiritual connection and see things. I don't know how or why."

"Maybe the how or why isn't important."

Suddenly, Winifred Evans turned her head toward Jay. "How did your family die?"

Caught completely by surprise, Jay yanked the reins of his horse. The animal stopped instantly and protested loudly.

"I'm sorry." She turned away. "I didn't mean to pry."

For a moment, Jay sat still and searched his inner self for the will to share his past with this gifted woman who already knew too much. No one knew him, and he wanted to keep it that way.

"My family and my past are private," Jay said coldly as he kicked the horse into motion again.

In his heart, Jay knew he had nothing to fear from Miss Evans. What he feared was inside himself—his own past, his own memories. For the last ten years, he'd run from the past and had never taken the time to properly deal with the pain and the tragedy. He had lived the first few years of his life in the forests of southern Kentucky, barely a stone's throw from the Cumberland River. When he and his sister were denied entry into school, his father had moved the family west across the Mississippi River, into southern Missouri where Colored children and White children attended school together. Education, his father claimed, was the only way for Colored children to make something of themselves in the world instead of being servants all their lives.

One day, young Jason Peares returned from hunting for the family's winter food supply only to find his home burned to the ground and his family murdered. When the local sheriff offered no help to find the murderers, young Jason Peares rode off by himself, tracking the killers. He thought that if he found them, he could have them arrested.

He found them in Malden, Missouri. The local sheriff there told him bluntly that no White men would hang on the word of a Negro.

So Jason Peares brought frontier justice to the five killers himself. Accidentally. When he confronted the killers, they drew down on him. He panicked and pulled his father's ancient six-shooter from his belt and shot all but one of the killers dead.

The bigoted sheriff of Malden took exception to a Black man killing White men, even men who arguably deserved it, and put a price on Jason's head. Because of the Malden shootout, young Jason quickly became known as a larger-than-life gunfighter, and he then spent the next four years running in the night and hiding in the day as the price on his head grew from fifty dollars to hundreds of dollars.

When he was nineteen years old, he'd met an old railroad worker named Liu Wang. Jason was a wandering lad from a sheltered life, trying to survive the hard frontier life. He was losing and Liu Wang saw this. He taught young Jason the mental and physical skills he needed to survive. He also taught Jason how to avoid trouble—most times without killing—and how to deal with it effectively when it could not be avoided.

Wang also taught him self-defense. Jason possessed a natural skill at gun handling. He was quick on the draw and extremely accurate, but Wang showed him how to use a knife and his hands and feet for silent defense, so he could take care of himself in any situation.

Over the years, Jason had escaped several bounty hunters and lawmen, and the price for his capture continued to climb. Finally, he grew weary of the running and hiding, tired of wondering who might recognize him, or which of his handful of friends would shoot him in the back or turn him over to the law for a handful of gold. When confronted by a posse of detectives from the Pinkerton National Detective Agency, he chose to avoid a bloody gunfight. He surrendered.

To his surprise, he was acquitted of all charges after a witness to the original shooting testified he'd shot in self-defense.

Jason had been set free, but he knew it would be many months before all those still searching for him would hear the news. Meanwhile, he decided to shorten his name to Jay and drop his surname.

Occasionally, people recognized him. They came after him, either for the old bounty, not knowing he was no longer an outlaw, or because he had killed their kinfolk. Sometimes another gunfighter simply wanted to make a reputation for himself by challenging him. There seemed to be nowhere that was safe.

In time, everyone who had ever gotten close to him had his or her lives touched by violence. He did not want Miss Evans to share that fate.

Their ride ended as Jay pulled his horse up to Miss Evans's one-room shack in the middle of a small empty valley ten miles southeast of Bronco. The shack was barely sturdy enough to keep out the wind and rain. It had a single window and a vent for the stovepipe. All in all, it looked like a comfortable home. Certainly, it was more than what he possessed. While nothing but weeds and scrub grass seemed able to grow in the whole valley, a small garden flourished beside the shack to provide some food.

Jay pulled up to the front door, dismounted, then helped Miss Evans down. She held his hand for a moment, then squeezed slightly before releasing it.

"Visit with me again sometime?" she said.

"I will. And I'm sorry about being rude. My past is a touchy subject, that's all."

Winifred Evans smiled. "You let me hold your hand. You didn't pull away. That told me all I need to know."

He said nothing.

"You're a strange young man, Jay. I know you're educated because you speak to me in proper English, and you seem gentlemanly." She smiled briefly for a moment, then the smile faded. "Yet you speak to Pritchett and his men in language they can understand." She paused. "You are full of pain and frustration."

"That's how you see me?"

"I see that you're ruthless, even deadly, when someone crosses you. But you can be tender when you need to be. And I see new love blossoming in your heart for the woman."

"What woman?"

She merely smiled and continued. "But there's something wrong, some barrier between you two. And Pritchett is not your friend. There is something big and dark and deadly in your future with him."

CHAPTER 4

PATRICK SPENCER AWOKE EARLY MONDAY morning with a start. The homesteader opened his eyes wide, at first confused that sunlight brightened the room. Then he remembered today was his youngest son's fourth birthday. Patrick and his wife had stayed up late preparing a special surprise for Michael. As a result, he had overslept.

Spencer rolled out of bed, careful not to wake his wife. He crept into the next room and watched Michael and the two middle children sleeping. He noted with pride that the fourth bed was empty. Henry, the oldest, was already up and outside doing his chores.

He yawned again and ruffled his hair as he walked out the back door toward the outhouse. Then he froze. Henry lay sprawled in the dirt halfway between the house and the outhouse. The dirt under his head was stained dark with his blood.

Spencer screamed for his wife to wake up, then ran out to his son. He rolled Henry over and stared into the boy's lifeless eyes. Spencer's gaze was slowly drawn to the deep gash on the side of Henry's head. Someone had hit him with something, hard.

Spencer started to rise just as the shadow passed over him. He froze, feeling the cold metal of a gun against the base of his skull. He never heard the gunshot that killed him.

The meeting to prepare for the ride out to the Hopkins property was not what Jay expected. He met Chuck Peters at the saloon just before sunrise, along with Slade and a new man he hadn't seen before named Paul Cranston. Pritchett, Bull, and Eddie Platt were absent from the meeting and the survey trip.

Peters poured himself and the three men a round of whiskey. When Slade and Jay refused their drinks, Peters drained the extra glasses. The only instruction he gave the men was a gruff, "Follow me," as he stomped out of the saloon. The rest of the trip passed without comment.

Jay checked his guns yet again as he and the three riders approached the first property they were to survey. On impulse, he checked the two spare guns in his saddle pack to make sure they were loaded. He didn't know why he checked them. He just had a feeling, and long ago he had learned to trust his feelings.

The four riders slowed as they neared the gate marking the front yard of the house. They entered single-file. Peters, Slade, and Cranston headed straight for the front door as if they owned the place. Jay approached slowly, sizing up the property and the surrounding area. He scanned the yard quickly, noting all the possible hiding places or ambush spots.

The yard was large, about 200 feet from the gate to the house and twice that distance in width. The fence stretched around the house on three sides, leaving the back of the house open to the field beyond. On the left half of the yard, well-tended green grass extended from the front door all the way to the gate and away to the left boundary fence.

About 100 feet away from the left side of the house, next to the fence, was the small family grave plot with three grave markers. The right side of the yard was dirt and scrub grass for horse and buckboard traffic. The fence stretched away to the right for another 300 feet, then cut south and ended even with the back of the house. A barn stood at the front right corner of the yard, sided by a small corral that surprisingly held no horses.

The house was a large two-level structure with the door off-center. The right side and the whole second floor had probably been added on because the logs were of a different kind of tree and looked newer. A large glass windowpane took up most of the front wall to the left of the door. The drapes were drawn, and the door was open just an inch. Jay figured someone with a shotgun watched from behind that door.

A man stood holding a broom on the front porch, about twelve feet to the right of the door. The only other sign that anyone was home was a lone figure working behind a mule and plow far out in the distance.

The farmer was a tall Black man with graying hair, probably in his mid-fifties. He was bare-chested, showing a lean muscular torso. His dark skin glistened with sweat under the hot morning sun. Peters got down from his horse and walked up onto the porch to face the farmer.

"Mornin', Hodges," Peters said, his voice deep and rumbling in a slow Texas drawl.

"It's Hopkins. What you fellas want here?" the farmer replied.

Jay watched the farmer study the group. There was fierce defiance in his eyes, despite being outgunned five pistols and three Winchesters to one broom. There was a hint of something else too. Jay had seen the look before, many times. The farmer was willing to die for what he believed in.

Jay saw recognition in the man's eyes also when his gaze locked onto Jay. Hopkins looked away quickly to cover his discomfort, his fear. Jay had seen that look before too. Although Jay did not consider himself to be a gunfighter, he knew others did, and many people feared him because of this.

"We want to look at your property," Peters continued. "We're filing an assessment of all the squatters' places in this area so Mr. Pritchett can buy you out at a fair price, maybe even better than fair. And we have legal papers that say we can do it."

Peters removed a thick roll of maps from his back pocket and waved them in the air for emphasis.

"You got no right to come around here botherin' me and my family. And you can tell Pritchett again that I ain't sellin'. Now git."

"Don't get in our way, old man. We got us a new Negro here who Mr. Pritchett pays to keep the peace, if you know what I mean." Peters nodded toward Jay. "He calls himself Jay, and I'd think twice before causin' trouble if I was you, Hodges."

Again Hopkins studied Jay, his forearm muscles bulging as his grip tightened on the broomstick. Jay returned the farmer's stare for a moment more before glancing away, toward the door. Jay looked back at Hopkins and twitched the corner of his mouth as he moved his left hand closer to his holster. He was giving Hopkins a clear warning that he knew someone was behind the door.

The farmer sidestepped around Peters and placed himself between the door and Jay.

"Look, boys," Hopkins said, looking at Jay. "I don't want no trouble. We ain't hurtin' nobody. We're just tryin' to live. So, git off my property and leave us alone. Please."

Peters just snorted his contempt. "Sorry, *Hodges*." He emphasized the incorrect name. "We got ourselves a job to do." He turned back to his horse. "Let's do it, boys." He took half a step when Hopkins reached out and grabbed his shoulder.

"I said git off my property, now!"

Peters spun around savagely, breaking Hopkins' grip. He lashed out with the thick roll of maps in his left hand and jabbed at Hopkins' shoulder with such force that the farmer had to take a step back.

"I told you we got a legal court order here. It's signed by Judge Parrish and the sheriff," Peters said, waving the maps around again. "So you just stay out of my way." Chuck Peters paused and took a deep breath. "And, if you ever even think about putting your Black hand on me again, I'm gonna cut it off at the elbow."

Peters grinned, tapped Hopkins lightly on the cheek with the map roll, and turned to his horse. Jay saw the boy an instant before the boy launched his attack.

"You leave my grandpa alone!" squealed a tiny voice, high-pitched and full of anger.

Hopkins called the little boy and reached out for him, but the boy ran straight at Peters, swinging and kicking. Jay judged him to be about four years old and knew he could do no damage, but he was defending his grandfather. Peters stepped back from the pesky attack on his leg, but the little boy kept swinging.

"Git away, boy!"

Peters roughly swept his right boot sideways and caught the boy in the chest, knocking him over. At the same time, the door burst open, and Jay saw the woman from the church lunge outside, screaming the boy's name. In her right hand, she held a double-barreled shotgun.

Peters turned at the sound of Hopkins coming toward him and poised his right hand over his gun. The woman scooped up the boy with her free arm and dashed back through the door.

"Go 'head, mister," Peters snarled. "I'll kill you without thinking twice."

The woman put the boy down and started to raise the shotgun, but not before the boy raced past her and ran at Peters again. The woman and Hopkins both screamed "Jeremiah," but it was too late.

In the blink of an eye, Peters stepped back and raised the roll of maps to swing at the little boy. Hopkins reached for the broom by the door. The woman screamed and brought the shotgun up.

Everyone jumped at the sound of Jay's gunshot. Peters lurched sideways as wood exploded at his feet. Jeremiah jumped back, and the woman grabbed him and threw him bodily into the house. She ran in behind him, using her body as a shield, and slammed the door.

To Jay's left, Cranston had started to reach for his gun, but stopped when he realized Jay's second gun was leveled in his direction. Next to Cranston, Slade calmly patted his horse's neck.

After a moment, Peters recovered and stared at one of Jay's guns pointing at his head. Hopkins nervously eyed Jay's other gun as it slowly wavered to cover both Cranston and himself.

"Everybody relax," Jay commanded. "You, Hopkins, put that

broom down." He motioned his gun menacingly at the man. "And you, Peters. Back off."

Neither man moved so Jay cocked both his guns. "I'm not gonna ask you fellas again to be peaceable. Now move!"

After a few seconds, Hopkins took a few steps back and laid the broom against the wall. Peters stepped toward Jay.

"What the hell's the matter with you?" Peters shouted with anger. "You're supposed to be on our side!"

"Like you said, Pritchett pays me to keep the peace. I'm keepin' it. We didn't come out here to beat up on little kids."

"You'll regret this, Jay," Peters stammered. "No one crosses me and lives to talk about it."

"I'm not crossing you, Mr. Peters. I'm just keeping the peace." He holstered his guns and slid down from his horse. "Let's just get on with our survey and leave these people alone."

As soon as Jay started to turn toward the porch, he saw movement to his left.

Paul Cranston again went for his gun but froze in the middle of his motion when he saw that Jay had outdrawn him. Jay glanced over at Slade, who kept his left hand clear from his gun. As Jay looked back at Cranston, he saw Chuck Peters out of the corner of his eye going for his gun. Jay drew his right pistol and had his gun pointed and cocked before Peters even had his grabbed properly.

"Look, Mr. Peters. I'm trying real hard not to kill you," Jay said quietly. "But you're making it mighty difficult. Now, I said back off, and I mean just that. If we have to discuss this again, the talkin' won't be done with words. Next time I have to pull my gun, you're gonna be a dead man. I hope you understand me clearly."

Peters stepped back quickly and raised his hands away from his gun belt in surrender. Jay nodded and put both his guns away.

"Now that we have some peace," Jay said calmly, "why don't you fellas head on back to town and let me do the surveys."

He stepped over to the porch and held out his hand to Peters for the roll of maps. Peters stepped forward and tossed the roll down at Jay's feet. Jay smiled and bent down to get the roll. At the same time, Peters's knee rammed up toward Jay's face.

Jay had seen the intent in Peters's eyes long before the man moved. Jay reached under his right pants leg for his buffalo bone hunting knife. As he bent down, he pivoted to his right and leaned forward, inside Peters' kick. He knocked the leg aside and rose up to his full height beside Peters.

Jay caught him under the chin with his left hand, bringing the man upright as he stepped in close. He brought the blade up to the man's neck. Slowly and deliberately, he moved the flat side of the blade against Peters's throat as the man trembled in fear.

Behind Jay, Cranston went for his gun a third time, slowly and quietly. Almost quietly, but not quietly enough. Jay heard the rub of metal on leather and turned his head sideways as Slade reached out to grab Cranston's arm. Cranston looked at the man beside him, and Slade shook his head. Jay met Slade's gaze for a second. Then he shoved Peters toward his horse and backed up to face all three men.

"Ride out," he said simply. Again he looked at Slade. "You too."

Slade eyed Jay for long seconds after Chuck Peters pulled himself onto his horse. Even as Peters and Cranston turned to leave, Jay knew Slade was debating whether or not to answer the challenge. Slade stared at him for a moment, then simply smiled and turned his horse away.

But the look in Slade's eyes as he turned his horse was unmistakable. Jay had seen it too many times before to ignore it this time. Slade was completely under control. The time would soon come when Slade would answer the challenge, and one of them would die.

CHAPTER 5

J AY WATCHED THE THREE MEN pass through the gate, then picked up the roll of maps and turned to face Hopkins.

"Mr. Hopkins, I—"

"If you're expecting any kind of thanks, well, you can just forget it. Now get off my property."

"Mr. Pritchett has the legal right to survey your land and that of the other squatters in this area. And you can see he's ready to use force."

"Squatters, hell! I've been here for nineteen years. I built this house all by myself and went and cut down every tree to do it. I'll die before I let anybody take it from me or run me off."

Jay unrolled the maps and read them for a moment. Then he told Hopkins, "Court records show you've been here less than five years. I've got a copy here. And they're signed by a judge from another county. There's no way Pritchett can buy a judge, if that's what you're thinking."

"Pritchett owns the town, the sheriff, and everybody else that matters. Maybe he just had them papers changed. It don't make no difference anyhow. I'm here, I've been here, and I'm stayin' here."

Jay studied Hopkins as the big farmer studied him. Hopkins stood with his hands on his hips, and Jay knew the mere fact that he worked for Pritchett was threatening to Hopkins. Yet he sensed that the man was looking for a compromise.

"Mr. Hopkins, can you prove you've been here longer than five years?"

"Aw, I don't know." Hopkins scratched his head and kicked at the porch flooring. "A lot of people know we been here."

"Other squatters...er...homesteaders?"

"Yeah, I guess so."

"Any proof would have to be able to stand up in court, not just other people in the same situation as you. The court will assume all your friends and common associates will support your story, and all Pritchett's people will back him. But Pritchett has documented papers, so that gives him the advantage. I suspect he has a lot more money to waste on lawyers and such too."

"Ain't no law or lawyers to help people like us."

Jay stared at the farmer for a moment. He didn't like what the man was implying. "The law is the law," Jay said a bit too harshly. "Don't matter what color you are."

"I'm not talking about color, son. There's more than twenty farming families around this county—Black, White, and Mexican. We all got the same problem with Pritchett. Fact is, you're working for Pritchett, and he's takin' our land. He's paying gunfighters to take what don't belong to him. Law or no law, that ain't right."

Jay took a deep breath. "Well, regardless of who's right or wrong, if someone in your family would help me survey your property, maybe we can find something that'll prove your claim and will stand up in court. We have nothing to lose that wouldn't be lost without trying."

"Well, all right. I don't suppose it'll do any harm. I'll tell Belle to show you whatever you gotta see. Just stay out of the garden." Hopkins paused. "Might even stop some of this trouble that's brewing. And keep some people from dying." As an afterthought, he added, "Might've been some today."

Jay watched Hopkins turn and walk into the house. He felt the warmth of his small victory, but Hopkins's gratitude was about the most stubborn *thank you* he'd ever heard. He chuckled and rolled up the scroll of papers, except for the map of the

Hopkins farm, then hoisted himself up onto his horse. He stuck the rest of the maps in his saddlebag and started the horse slowly around the right side of the house.

As Jay started looking around, he noticed little things that seemed out of place for a house that was less than five years old as the map indicated. This was a home, not just a house. The windows all had decorative shutters on the outside, and the sloped roof had gutters to direct rainwater into the flower bushes along the sides of the house. The porch railings and posts had been nicely lathed and finished.

Jay knew it was hardly possible that a hardworking man could have built all the extra niceties and conveniences he saw within five years, and still have earned a living. Maybe there was something to Hopkins's claim after all. And that grave plot bothered Jay too. If any of those three folks had died more than five years ago, the family must have been at the homestead at least that long. Nobody digs up graves and moves them to another homestead.

As Jay rode around to the back of the house, he saw a standard clothesline made of two T-shaped wooden posts with bale wire strung in between. There was the outhouse, located a few yards from the back door, and what looked like a tool shed. Closer inspection revealed several foot-powered woodworking tools for use in crafting furniture and such.

He also noticed an odd-looking windmill. As he looked closer, Jay saw the windmill was hooked to a modified water hand-pump. The outlet pipe from the pump was extended and went straight into the ground. The other end of that pipe came up out of the ground next to the house, rising up into the wall to supply water inside the house. A valve fed a small pipe leading around to the front of the house, no doubt to irrigate the green grass, Jay realized. Hopkins had found a way to let the wind pump water into the house, more like the kind of convenience one installed after living the hard way for so long.

Jay's concentration was interrupted by the sound of a squeaking door opening and closing. He turned his horse around, and there stood the woman he'd seen in town yesterday. He'd barely seen her as she'd dashed onto the front porch to grab the boy, but now he gazed at the whole woman long enough to see that she was very pretty.

She stood there staring at him from the porch step with her arms folded across her front impatiently. Her dark brown skin contrasted sharply with the bright yellow of her summer dress. The bright dress made her look stunningly beautiful.

Her eyes took his breath away. They were large and dark and beautiful, but at the same time they were very unfriendly.

"What are you gapin' at?" she demanded.

"You must be Belle," he said aloud.

"My name is Marabelle, but my friends call me Belle," she answered. "You can call me Miss Hopkins."

Jay just smiled slightly. "Will you be showing me your property?"

"Pa told me to show you whatever you have to see for your survey."

"Well, whenever you're ready, I'd like to get started. I have two other places—"

"Just give me a minute to change," she said, turning for the door.

Her words were sharp, but Jay knew a pound of sugar could sweeten even the sourest spice.

"By the way, Miss Hopkins," Jay said before the door closed. "My name is Jay." He smiled more noticeably this time.

"I know," she said through the screen door. Her dark eyes drilled into his. "I heard the introduction. You're Mr. Pritchett's new Negro."

Jay's eyes flared as she spun away from the door. He closed his eyes and took a deep breath, trying to shrug off the cutting insult. He reined his horse around angrily to continue his survey, but the animal protested loudly.

"Sorry 'bout that, ol' girl."

Jay ducked under the clothesline and studied the map for a long minute. He was just about to fold it away when he heard the crunching sound. As he reined up, he looked down. His horse was several steps into rows of turnip greens and something else that looked like the tops of carrot stalks. If he could just back out the way he came and fix it real quick, he could act like nothing ever happened.

From behind him, someone said, "Boy! I'm gonna bust this here broom over yo' head if you don't git yo' butt out of my vegetables!"

Jay looked around to see a short dark-skinned woman storming toward him. She looked about fifty and wielded a straw-tipped house broom. Jay hurried out of the vegetable patch and dismounted to apologize.

"I'm sorry, I—" he began.

"Sorry, my foot, boy! I don't break my back every day out here just for some young gunfighter to come and stomp all through it. Now go git that hoe from over yonder and git to work, 'fore I go upside yo' head."

"Look, lady, I—" Jay jumped as the little woman brought the broom hard against his left hip.

"Don't you 'look lady' me, 'cause I ain't yo' lady!"

Jay stepped toward the woman and reached for the broom, but she just slapped his hand away with her free hand and continued.

"Boy, don't you dare to raise a hand at me! I'll beat you from here to Missour-uh!" She was shouting now. "Just because you're wearing guns, don't mean you can't be whupped!"

Jay towered over the little woman by a foot and a half, so she poked him repeatedly in the lower chest with a bony index finger as she lectured.

"Now, you best do what I tol' you, and do it now!"

"Look, I've had just about enough—"

Jay jumped as the broom landed with a solid whack against his left thigh.

"I'll tell you when you done had enough. When you fix my vegetables and learn some manners. *Then* you had enough!"

She swung and hit twice more. Jay cursed and grabbed

the woman's arm. He had never raised his hand to a woman and wasn't about to start now, but it was time to end this. He reached for the broom, but she pulled him forward off-balance. The hard straw slammed into the side of his face and again on the back of his head.

He flinched and blinked, protecting his head with his arms, but she smacked him hard on the side of his face, then poked him in the belly, and on the head again.

"All right, all right!" He stumbled away, but she half-chased him to the side of the house where the garden hoe lay. Jay saw Hopkins standing at the back door, rifle in hand and smiling.

"I see you've met my wife, Miss Clara. She's not afraid of gun-fighters."

"I ain't no gunfighter," Jay said harshly as he snatched the hoe from where it leaned against the wall. He jumped as Miss Clara whacked him against the butt with the broom.

"I didn't ask you to do no talkin', did I?"

Jay cringed with embarrassment and helplessness as Hopkins laughed. Miss Clara followed Jay back to the vegetable patch, lecturing him all the while on elders and manners. He hadn't let anyone talk to him like this ever before in his adult life.

"And where you from, anyway, thinkin' you can back-talk women? Hmmm? Answer me, boy! Didn't yo' mama teach you no manners? Let me tell you, if I heard my boy was off back-talking his elders, I'd be takin' a branch to his backside. I got half a mind to light into you again, rude as you are."

The scolding lasted until Jay had repaired the damage done by his horse.

"Good. That's better. Now go on 'bout yo' biz'ness."

As Miss Clara turned abruptly and headed back to the house, Jay saw that Hopkins was no longer at the door. Jay retrieved his hat from the dirt and beat it against his leg while turning to get his horse. Marabelle stepped out the door and held it open for her mother, then turned toward Jay. The embarrassing moment faded as he walked his horse over to her, all the while studying her and noting every detail.

She was about five and a half feet tall and wore a pair of skin-tight corduroys with a man's light brown shirt printed with dark brown boxes. She was a full-figured woman, by far the finest woman Jay had ever seen. She had shoulder-length hair as black as midnight tied back in a single ponytail. Her eyes were bright and beautiful, but her stare was still mean.

"Well?"

"Sorry, ma'am," Jay said, turning to fidget with his horse. "I didn't mean to stare. It's just...."

"Just what? You never seen a woman before?"

"None so beautiful."

She hesitated for a moment, surprised by his words.

"You sure got your nerve, mister. I'm not interested in hearing your compliments."

Jay simply looked at her, tried and failed to keep a neutral expression on his face. "Why are you so angry with me?" He flung his arms up in exasperation.

"Why am I angry?" she repeated. She took a step closer as if to confront him with the obvious. "You and your men ride in here and threaten us and stomp all over our privacy, pull your guns and bully your way past my father, and kick my son around. And you wonder why I'm angry?"

"If I hadn't stopped them—"

"You're Pritchett's gunfighter. And I know if we don't do what he says, he'll have us killed. He's said as much before."

Jay narrowed his eyes at Marabelle's allegations. He hesitated a moment, finally understanding her anger. Pritchett had the money and legal papers to stake unclaimed land that the squatters were occupying. Since Jay worked for Pritchett, that made him the enemy.

"I'm not a gunfighter," he said quietly. "Mr. Pritchett hired me to keep the peace, and that's what I intend to do. Maybe you didn't see, but if I hadn't intervened out there," he gestured toward the front of the house, "your pa would probably be dead right now, and your son—"

"I saw. But you got no right forcing your way onto our property."

Jay realized then why Pritchett needed a peacekeeper. If all the squatters were as belligerent as the Hopkins family was, then Jay and the rest of the surveyors would face resistance, even violence, at every farm. Left on their own, Peters and the others would answer the farmers' protests with deadly force.

He knew he'd have to patch things up with Chuck Peters. He acknowledged that making an enemy of Peters, or any of Pritchett's men, wasn't exactly the smartest course of action. He might need them to watch his back if the farmers became violent.

Suddenly, Jay became aware of a dull pain in the left side of his face where Miss Clara had whacked him. He just wasn't having much luck with the Hopkins women.

"Well, let's get this survey done, if you don't mind. You got a horse?"

"Horse?" Marabelle stepped back with her hands on her hips. "You see any horses around here?" Jay glanced around, wondering where the animals might be. "You and your men stole all our horses. We had to borrow a mule just so we could plow the field."

"I don't know anything about—"

"Oh, sure. Maybe you should ask Mr. Pritchett. We know it was him."

Jay grew tired of the confrontation. He lifted himself into the saddle and looked down at Marabelle. He'd had enough of her scorn.

"Miss Hopkins, you're entitled to think whatever you want of me. When I saw you in town yesterday, I was hoping we might get acquainted a bit, but now I see that's pretty much impossible. But I'm gonna tell you one thing about me. I don't shoot unarmed men, and I don't bully people around or kick little kids.

If I see anyone misbehaving like that, I'll have words about it, whether I work with him or not.

"I haven't been in town a whole day yet, and I don't know anything about any stolen horses. Hell, I thought surveying was just going to be an easy job. I'm not even sure I want to stay around and get wrapped up in all this mess."

"Even if you ride off, Mr. Pritchett will just hire another gun-fighter."

Jay cocked his eyebrow at her.

"Peacekeeper," she said quickly. "I meant he'll hire another peacekeeper."

Jay nodded. "Well, I just stayed in town because of what Miss Evans said."

"The Witch Lady? What did she say?"

Jay hesitated for a second. "She hinted that there was something special...." His breath caught, and he cleared his throat.

"Well? Special about what?"

"About you." Jay turned away, embarrassed, and patted his horse's rump. "Come on. Let's ride."

She climbed up. "What else did she say?"

He shrugged. "She wasn't clear on details."

Jay spurred the horse into a slow trot. They didn't talk, but Marabelle surprised him by wrapping both arms around him to hold on. She leaned in close, bouncing roughly from riding on the horse's rump.

Jay could feel the pressure of her body against his back. Her closeness and motion aroused him considerably. It had been nearly a year since he'd been with a woman and several years before that since he'd been in love. He found himself wondering about Marabelle, wondering things that men always seem to wonder about when close to a woman. For a while, he enjoyed pretending she didn't hate him.

CHAPTER 6

J AY AND MARABELLE TOOK ALMOST half an hour to reach the field where her brother worked the plow. He stopped working as Jay and Marabelle rode up. Daniel was dark-skinned like the rest of the family and was stocky and muscular like his father. Except for the straw hat he wore to shade his eyes from the sun's glare, Daniel was naked from the waist up.

The instant Jay looked into Daniel's eyes, he sensed he had seen the young man somewhere before. Daniel nodded a wordless greeting.

"Daniel, this is Jay," Marabelle said. "He came out to survey our land."

"You make your surveys with guns?" Daniel said quietly, eyeing the double-gun holster.

"No, today I'm using a map."

Jay stretched out his hand. Daniel returned the handshake, and both men sized each other up with a firm grip.

"So why do you need those guns? Seems fairly peaceful around here."

"They come in handy every now and again. I've been hired to keep the peace between the homesteaders and Pritchett's men. Can't very well keep the peace without guns."

Daniel turned up the side of his mouth in a sneer. "Who hired you?"

"Jay's doin' the surveys for the land office," added Marabelle.

She released her grip on Jay's waist and tapped a warning on his thigh.

Daniel ignored his sister. "I asked who hired you."

Jay hesitated for a moment. He was trying to figure out what the warning was for and at the same time trying to recall where he'd met Daniel.

"I'm working for Pritchett. You have a problem with that too?"

He did. Daniel's hazel eyes narrowed as he took steps toward Jay's horse. To Jay's surprise, Marabelle spoke again in his defense.

"Now just a minute, Daniel. Jay stopped Chuck Peters from hitting Jeremiah and starting trouble with Pa. He's just—"

"He works for Pritchett. That's enough for me." Daniel turned his attention to Jay. "And if you think I'm gonna let you ride off with my sister, you got another thing comin'."

"Your father asked her to show me around."

"Yeah, well, he ain't here, and what I say goes. And she ain't goin' with you."

"I think—"

"Both of you just quit your fussin'," interrupted Marabelle. "I'm a big girl, Daniel, and I'm the elder, so what I say goes. Besides, I can take care of myself. Nothing's gonna happen to me."

"Nothin' better not happen to her, or you'll wish you were dead," Daniel added quietly. Jay was unmoved by the threat.

"Only way I'd let anything happen to her is if I'm already dead or close to it."

The two men stared at each other. Jay broke the silence.

"I don't suppose you've ever been up in New Mexico or Colorado?"

"No, why?"

"How about the Indian Territories?"

"You mean that area they call Oklahoma? Naw."

"I'm sure I've seen you somewhere before. I thought it might have been somewhere north of here."

"If it wasn't here, it wasn't nowhere," returned Daniel. "Because I ain't been out of this part of Texas."

"Well, I guess I'm mistaken."

Jay knew there was no mistake. Daniel was too familiar. Sometime in the past few years he'd seen those eyes somewhere before. He let it pass. It would come to him in time. He spurred his horse, and he and Marabelle rode toward the hills southwest of the field where Daniel worked. Jay angled his head back to speak to Marabelle.

"I guess Daniel doesn't like Mr. Pritchett much either."

"Not many people do. He's taking everyone's property."

"You know that's just one side of a two-sided argument."

"To us and others like us who'll lose everything we own, there's only one side. And Pritchett's not on it. Besides, I tried to warn you."

"I've never been one to dodge the truth."

"Well, even though I'm older than him by six years—"

"How old are you, anyway?"

"Twenty-five. And you?"

"Twenty-seven." He paused. "You were saying?"

"I was saying that even though I'm older than Daniel, he wants to protect me because I'm a woman."

"Can't fault him for that. You're certainly worth protecting."

"Worth dying for, like you told my brother?"

Jay hesitated for a moment. He didn't know why he'd said that, but he knew he meant it. There was something special about this woman.

"Yes, but I hope I won't have to die to prove my words or my intentions," he said and chuckled.

"Intentions? And just what intentions might those be?"

Jay cringed inside, mentally admonishing himself for letting a childish fantasy interfere with business. The woman hated him and what he represented. Nothing could be clearer. Caught with his guard down, Jay just shrugged.

"Well, like I told him, I'm quite capable of taking care of myself." Almost as an afterthought, she added, "Even with you."

"Is that so?" Jay said, annoyed at her overconfidence.

"Yep," she answered a bit too cheerfully. "That's so."

"Well, if I were you and saw what you saw on your front porch, I wouldn't be so sure of myself."

Immediately, Jay regretted his harsh words. After the reception he had received, though, he knew it wouldn't matter. Miss Evans was wrong about Marabelle. Or maybe he had just misunderstood her because his heart was stricken. He took a deep breath and sat straighter in the saddle. It was time to tend to business and stop fantasizing like a lovestruck kid.

Jay knew he had chilled Marabelle's spirits, but he welcomed the silence and studied the terrain around him. The field Daniel was working in stretched almost to the base of the ridge of low hills four miles south of the house and followed the hill for about six miles to the Hopkins's west border.

The field was divided into two sections by a wide corridor for traffic to the valley beyond the hill. Marabelle commented that they kept two dozen cows grazing in the east end of the valley and about half a dozen bundles of grain for them to eat during these hot summer months. Jay would have to note all these details on the map so an accurate worth of the property could be assessed.

Jay paused at the top of the hill to look back over the land behind them. This was a near-perfect location for a homestead. He could see the house in the distance, and he looked over the field stretching off to a narrow ribbon of trees that lined the creek on the west property border. To the north of the farm lay the empty stretch of land almost completely devoid of everything except sticker bushes and scrub grass. Everything else from the creek to the hill where they now sat, then off to the east edge of the farm where the hill turned to the north and gently sloped into the flatland, was living and growing. Again, Jay found it hard to believe the Hopkinses could take useless land and carve life and food from it in less than five years. He turned the horse back to the south and rode down into the valley to find the cattle.

The valley was about 300 yards wide and was covered with

sparse green grass. There were no cattle, so they rode up the valley to the east and north. They both saw the massacre at the same time. The cattle lay scattered around the valley, and the six huge bundles of grain stood in scorched ruin.

"Still think Mr. Pritchett is a good boss?" Marabelle asked. "He did this, you know."

"I don't know any such thing." He paused. "And I never claimed he was a good boss."

Jay guided the horse slowly toward the dead animals, glancing around for signs of the responsible person or persons. He stopped and dismounted, then walked among the carcasses. The stench was so bad he had to hold a kerchief to his nose. Still, the smell was nauseating, and he sucked air through his mouth to fight the sickness churning his stomach.

The ants and maggots had already set in, so he figured the animals had been dead for at least two days. Jay noticed some of the animals had only been shot in the legs or hindquarters and left to suffer a slow and agonizing death—a message to the owners.

There were several sets of horse prints around the area, but none were distinctly identifiable. Jay walked over to one of the charred bundles of grain and noticed a peculiar patch of ground that was burned brown but not charred black by fire. Kerosene. It was not enough to kill the cattle, but someone had gone to a lot of extra trouble to make sure none of the grain was left usable.

Jay stood up to return to his horse and Marabelle, then stopped. He looked back at the ground searching. He saw it in a passing glance, something different, something that didn't belong.

Then he found it, only a few paces to his left. The hoof that had made the print had a small hole almost exactly in the center of the curved horseshoe. He looked for and soon found the other three prints that a standing horse would make. Somewhere out there, probably in Bronco, was a horse with an abnormal front left shoe. When he found that horse, he would find the man responsible for this business.

Jay returned to his horse and offered the saddle to Marabelle, then climbed up behind her. They rode back up the corridor in silence, passing Daniel without stopping.

Jay slid down and helped Marabelle out of the saddle. He watched her disappear wordlessly into the house, then he turned as Mr. Hopkins walked around the far side of the house.

"Did you find anything interesting?" the farmer asked.

Jay nodded. "I saw a lot more than I should have for squatters who supposedly have been around here only for a couple of years," Jay said, looking at the windmill water pump.

"So you believe me."

"Yes, I do. Proving it might be difficult, though." He paused, then another idea struck him. "You know, if you had twelve smaller vanes on your windmill, instead of just those six, your pump would work a lot better. And if you mounted them at thirty degrees instead of forty-five, it would turn a lot faster."

Hopkins scratched the side of his head. "What the hell is thirty degrees?"

"That's one-third of a right cross and forty-five degrees is half of a right cross."

"Yeah? Well, how do you know it'll work better?"

"Because if you have more vanes, the wind has a larger target to hit, and if they're tilted at a third of a cross, rather than at half a cross, less wind will be wasted passing through, and then the windmill will turn faster and do more work."

"Where'd you learn all that from?"

"In school."

"You mean you got some book learnin'?" Hopkins exclaimed. "How the hell'd you get stuck out here packin' guns, then?"

"I guess life is kinda hard to shape the way you want it sometimes. Anyway, I have some bad news for you also. Looks like someone slaughtered your cows and burned your grain over yonder. I found—"

"He's gone too far this time," Hopkins said, turning away.

"I can find out who did it," Jay said.

"I know who did it—the man you work for. Now get off my property. You ain't welcome around here no more. I'll handle this myself." Hopkins stepped through the back door.

"You can't be sure—"

"I'm sure. Now git!" He slammed the door behind him.

Jay knew what would happen if Hopkins stormed into town looking for Pritchett, but there was no way he could stop the farmer. He pulled out the map and a pen and inkbottle from his pack, then made several notes. A few minutes later, Jay mounted up and reined his horse around to leave just as Miss Clara came around the west side of the house carrying a watering pot.

"Ma'am," he tipped his hat. "I'm sorry about earlier."

"I forgive you," she said. "But you might want to brush up on those manners."

"Yes, ma'am."

Jay rode around to the front of the house, not believing he had really apologized to someone. So much time had passed since he'd been around decent civilized folk, he'd forgotten how to act. Among the drifters and gunfighters he usually met or rode with, civilized manners were often considered a sign of weakness. Jay thought maybe he could enjoy not having to be so tough all the time.

Marabelle's voice interrupted his thoughts. "You don't seem like the kind of man that would take up with Mr. Pritchett's gang of gunmen and bullies." She stood on the front porch, watching him ride by.

"You don't think the others would have conducted a fair survey, do you?" he said, halting his horse.

She shook her head. "Did you make a fair survey?"

"I did."

"Mr. Pritchett doesn't care about fair surveys," she walked over to the near end of the porch. "And your survey isn't going to matter none, either."

"Then, why is he wasting time with these surveys if he doesn't plan to make a fair offer?"

"I don't know. But it doesn't matter what kind of offer he makes. Don't you understand? We don't want to sell. Not for any price."

The horse skittered restlessly, and Jay leaned forward and patted its neck. Marabelle stood leaning against the porch rail, arms folded across her stomach. Her expression had softened a bit and seemed less defiant.

"Don't you care that he's ruthless?" she asked finally, breaking the uncomfortable silence.

"Most businessmen are. Otherwise, they don't stay in business very long."

"I don't mean about business." She sighed in exasperation and grabbed the top of the rail with both hands. Her eyes implored him to listen to her. "He hires gunfighters to bully the farmers. You know what would have happened if you hadn't been here?"

"Your father started the trouble."

"How can you say that?"

Jay shrugged. "I can't say it's smart for one unarmed man to go against four armed men."

"But you all were trespassing."

"Still not good odds." Jay softened his voice. "I can show you the maps. They clearly show there are no claims or recorded deeds on any of this county land. That means we aren't trespassing. It's open land by law. You folks and other farmers built your houses on open land, without due process."

Marabelle raised her eyebrows. "All of us? All twenty-five farm families?"

"Actually, there are twenty-six families," Jay said. He shrugged almost apologetically. A flicker of irritation crossed Marabelle's face at the trivial point.

"Still," she said. "I can see some of us forgetting or not knowing how to register our claims, but not all of us. I wouldn't believe that's possible."

Jay considered the logic of her argument, then hesitantly argued. "It doesn't seem likely, I'll agree to that point, but when an area is ripe for settling, squatters rarely consider the legal, long-term consequences."

"And I'll agree to that point," she said, smiling. It occurred to Jay that she had intentionally cornered him into conceding her side of the debate. She continued.

"But squatters build one or two room cabins, knowing they'll have to pick up and move again in a year or two." She waved a hand around the porch and yard. "They don't build large houses with glass windows and rain gutters and windmill water pumps. And they don't plant shrubs and grass."

"I have to admit, for argument's sake, you have a good point."

"But it doesn't change anything, does it?"

"Not much."

"At least you listen to reason." Marabelle paused. "After surveying our land, are you comfortable calling us squatters?"

Jay hesitated. "To be truthful, I'm not real comfortable with that conclusion. No."

Marabelle reached to the other side of a nearby porch column and brought out a tall glass that Jay hadn't noticed from where he sat. She held the glass out to Jay.

"It's warm out here. Have some lemonade."

All of a sudden, Jay felt giddy. The hatred and anger had vanished from Marabelle's demeanor. He hadn't thought it possible that she would ever treat him nicely. He slid down from his horse and stepped over close to the porch. As he accepted the glass from her, their fingers touched, and Jay's heart jumped in his chest. She watched him as he drank the cool liquid, and he stared into her beautiful dark eyes.

Suddenly, Jay heard the pitter-patter of tiny boots and looked over Marabelle's shoulder to see little Jeremiah walking across the porch toward them. He leaned down and to his right and started to speak, but Jeremiah grinned bashfully behind Marabelle and snuck over to her other side.

Jay leaned over to his left, but again the boy grinned and moved behind Marabelle. This time, Jay quickly leaned to the right and was waiting for Jeremiah. The boy giggled and tried to hide again.

"I see you back there."

"Jeremiah, stop that," Marabelle said gently. "How are you supposed to meet people?"

The boy came out from behind his mother and held out his right hand. Jay responded and they shook.

"My name's Jeremiah."

"Pleased to make your acquaintance. I'm Jay."

"Are you gonna shoot your gun again?"

Jay glanced up at Marabelle, then squatted down and looked at Jeremiah through the porch rails.

"Did I scare you before?" The boy nodded. "Well, that man was going to hurt you and your grandpa, so I was just trying to scare *him*, not you. But I promise, I won't do it again. Okay?"

Jeremiah nodded and Marabelle said, "Go on inside, Jeremiah. I have to talk to Jay."

"Can I stay and talk too, Mama?"

Jay smiled at the boy. "You and I, we'll talk again, okay?"

"Okay." The boy turned and ran into the house.

"That's a fine-looking boy," Jay said, standing up. Now, he was uncomfortable with his feelings for this woman.

"His father took ill awhile back and...." She stared at Jay as if measuring his resolve. He couldn't think of anything appropriate to say, so he held her gaze and remained silent.

Marabelle changed the subject. "Your boss has gunmen out all over the county scaring and intimidating all the farmers. You've seen what they did to our grain and cattle. They're trying to scare us into moving away."

"Do you have proof?"

Marabelle shook her head and looked away to the north. It was then Jay got the uneasy feeling that she might be trying to manipulate him. He set the empty glass on the rail beside her and got on his horse, suddenly angry for allowing himself to be taken in by her charm.

"There's one problem with your reasoning, Miss Hopkins."

She smiled. "I'm sorry about earlier. Please, call me Marabelle."

He didn't. "If Pritchett was using scare tactics, he wouldn't need to be offering the farmers very reasonable prices for the land."

Behind Marabelle, Mr. Hopkins stepped out of the front door and walked toward them.

"You still here, boy? I told you to git!"

Jay nodded at Marabelle and tipped his hat. "Thank you for the lemonade, ma'am."

Jay spurred his horse into a trot and headed for the gate. Again, he noticed the family grave plot off to the right and cursed himself for forgetting to check the headstones. It was too late for that now, he figured, since he'd worn out his welcome with Mr. Hopkins.

Besides, he felt used and cheated. Marabelle had simply traded her anger for diplomacy, tried to plant a seed of doubt in his mind. Yet part of him wanted to turn around and look at her one last time. He was sure she would be watching him, savoring her victory, gloating in his feebleness. He had his pride. There was no way he would let her conquer that as well.

Jay considered his uncertain feelings for Marabelle, feelings he was quite sure she didn't share. He paused at the gate, fighting with conflicting thoughts and feelings.

To hell with pride, he thought. He turned in the saddle.

He saw Marabelle leaning against the porch rail, watching him. She raised her hand quickly to wave as if thinking he might turn away again and not see. He gazed at her for a long time. Finally, he put aside all the crazy thoughts of pride and manipulation. He smiled and waved, and she smiled back. Then he turned and rode away.

CHAPTER 7

S LADE WAITED FOR JAY HALF a mile outside the gate to Hopkins's property. Jay saw him as soon as he turned away from Marabelle. The man sat cool and controlled in his saddle, chewing on a stick of dried beef jerky, as Jay approached at a slow trot.

"Thought you'd be back in town by now," Jay said as he pulled his horse directly up in front of Slade's mount.

"I thought we'd better have a little chat before things get out of hand," Slade countered. He tore another bite of beef from the stick he held in his left hand.

Jay noted this and knew Slade wasn't looking for trouble. If he was, his left hand—his gun hand—would be free and clear. Jay pulled his horse alongside Slade's.

"All right, let's talk."

"Seein' as we're both on the same side here, it don't seem reasonable for us to end up at odds on the wrong end of a gun barrel." Slade paused to let his words sink in. "But the next time you challenge me like that," he nodded in the direction of the Hopkins farm, "you'd better be ready to back up your talk with gunplay."

"Are you threatening me?"

"Wouldn't waste my breath." Slade paused and spat juice off to the right. "Like you, I'm not one to be pushed, by hand or by word. Not by Pritchett or any of his hired guns, and not by you."

"I'll keep that in mind," Jay said simply.

Slade and Jay studied each other for long seconds. Prominent crow's feet framed Slade's blue eyes. His manner of confronting Jay showed he was a reasonable man and not insecure, arrogant, or afraid. Slade just sat there, chewing calmly on his jerky.

The man has an honest face, Jay thought, *and might be ten years older than me.*

"Is that all you wanted to talk about?" Jay said.

"I reckon that's the gist of it." Slade shrugged. "Just speakin' my mind is all."

Jay nodded. "I appreciate that."

Jay had met a lot of gunfighters. Very few of them ever backed down from a direct challenge. Some were always eager to prove their skills. Because they loved the thrill of winning so much, they figured it was worth the risk of losing. Still others couldn't back down because everyone was watching, and they feared humiliation more than death. A few didn't care who they fought because they didn't believe they could really be killed, or they didn't quite realize that death is the prize for second best. There were those who realistically knew there was always someone faster. They knew that someday, someone would come along to beat them. They accepted that reality and didn't worry about it. They were secure in their own abilities and let the opponent mind his own skills. They either quit being a gunfighter before they were killed, or they would be killed being a gunfighter.

Jay believed Slade belonged to the latter group. The man obviously didn't consider Jay a faster gun or else he wouldn't be talking with him. Neither would he underestimate Jay.

"Well," Jay said. "I don't suppose you have another piece of beef?" He eyed an oversized chunk sticking out of Slade's shirt pocket.

"I suppose I could spare a piece." Slade cut a small piece with a skinning knife retrieved from his belt, then handed the hard meat to Jay. "It's a bit salty, though."

Jay wrestled a bite. "So where do we go from here?" he asked, unsure of their truce.

"I suppose we could survey more farms."

"Sounds reasonable." They swung around and headed out to the west.

"By the way, Jay. Eddie Platt is not quite as compromising as you and me. I wouldn't mention it otherwise, but if you cross him, he'd just as likely shoot a man in the back as look at him. Just thought you might want to know."

"I'm grateful." Jay figured that was useful information, perhaps a gesture of friendship.

"I'm kinda curious, though. About why you didn't kill Chuck Peters awhile back. I would have, just to prove a point."

"The thought crossed my mind," Jay reflected. "I figured he'd be more valuable spreadin' the word about what happened. Might keep a few people off my back." He paused to take another bite of beef. "I sure would've killed Cranston if you hadn't stopped him from pulling that gun."

"Figured as much," Slade agreed. "I never gave no never mind about whether he lives or dies, but Hopkins was unarmed. Although I figure he might've done some damage with that broom handle. And that little boy was right there in the thick of things."

"I thought I was the only peacekeeper Pritchett had on his payroll."

"Mutual interest, I reckon." Slade tore off another bite. "Can't do much surveyin' with everybody killin' each other." He smiled.

"By the way," Jay asked innocently. "Have you heard any talk about farmers being threatened or forced out of the county? Maybe about stolen horses or mutilated cattle?"

"Can't say I have. Why do you ask?"

"I took some time to listen to how the farmers feel about Pritchett buying them out. Seems they're not too keen on the idea. They think Pritchett is using some underhanded scare tactics on some of the farmers."

"Well, I've only been on the payroll for about a month, but it doesn't seem reasonable that he'd be offering full value—sometimes more than full value—and jeopardizing his strategy by doing illegal activities at the same time."

"I had pretty much the same thoughts."

"Could just be angry squatters complaining because it's legal but not fair." Slade thought for a moment. "It's easy to see by the welcome we got back there that they're angry as hell about having to move. Throw someone abrasive like Chuck Peters into a situation like that, and I can understand why the farmers might say they're being intimidated or threatened."

"Yeah, that's probably all it is."

"I have to ask," Slade said quietly. "I know it's none of my business, but...."

"What's that?"

"I was just wondering what happened to your face?"

Jay rubbed his fingers along scratch marks that had not swollen yet but were still raw. He knew they probably showed a bit red.

"Bumped into a broom, that's all," Jay said shakily.

"Yeah?" Slade paused, then glanced at Jay sideways. "How many times?"

Slade said it innocently enough, but still Jay stopped his horse suddenly.

"You saw?"

"Reckon it's been awhile since I seen a two-gun-rig man taken down and whipped," Slade glanced over at Jay again and smiled devilishly. "And by an old lady with a broom!"

Slade broke out in great bellows of laughter, and Jay couldn't help but join in. They spent the four-hour ride to the next property in friendly conversation, and Jay felt that kindred spirit he'd thought about when he first saw Slade.

Pritchett finished his beer and began to consider what he wanted to eat for lunch. He absentmindedly watched the townsfolk stroll by on the boardwalk in front of the saloon window. They feared him, and that was exactly the response he wanted.

Pritchett had the power, and most people just stayed out of his way. They continued on about their business and followed his rules, knowing there was nothing they could do about him. That was why he wasn't overly concerned at the screaming protest of a horse and the sound of sliding wagon wheels, the clear indication that a rider had locked his wagon brakes with his horse running all out.

Pritchett knew Hopkins as a quiet man, more stubborn than most of the farmers and more adamant about refusing even to consider selling, but an honest and hardworking man. Pritchett always knew he would someday have to make a special example of him. Today was that day.

He'd never seen Hopkins fighting mad, but when Hopkins slammed through the saloon door, Pritchett saw hatred and murder in his eyes. Instantly, Pritchett knew Hopkins had found the dead livestock and ruined grain supply.

Ten men sat around the saloon drinking or talking about each other's mothers, but Hopkins paid them no attention. His focus centered on Pritchett sitting at the back of the room. Hopkins smiled as he held up his equalizer in his right hand, batting it solidly against his left palm.

Pritchett eyed the weapon, suddenly afraid for his life. The equalizer was a three-foot-long four-by-four with a smooth, rounded handle grip. At the square end, long roofing nails had been driven through each side, making the four-sided spiked end deadly no matter which side struck its target. Pritchett stood quickly, shouting for his bodyguard, Bull, who was in the outhouse.

Eddie Platt was sitting with a group of men at the table nearest the door and jumped up when Pritchett began shouting for Bull. He was quick to draw a gun, but Hopkins covered the short distance in a single step and elbowed the skinny man across the side of his head. Two other men tried to grab Hopkins's massive frame, but he shook them both off like flies. He clubbed one man with his equalizer, sending a spike into the man's skull. The other he sent toppling with a fist to his face.

Pritchett started to run toward the back door. Hopkins sidestepped the other men and cut him off. He grabbed the short man by the front of his white suit, lifted him bodily off the floor, and slammed him into the wall. He hesitated only a split second as he gazed into Pritchett's sinister brown eyes with total hatred, then he brought the equalizer down. Almost.

Four men jumped on Hopkins's back, literally dragging him away from Pritchett. One by one, he freed himself from the men, knocking most of them unconscious with his equalizer. Finally, Hopkins again turned in search of the man in white.

Pritchett stood against the back wall, and Hopkins approached slowly, as if wanting to savor the moment. That was his mistake. He had dropped his equalizer in his struggle with the last bunch of men and didn't bother to retrieve it for dealing with Pritchett. He was one step away from the man when the back door exploded open, and Bull charged in with the speed of a mountain lion. Hopkins turned to meet him, and the two men clashed.

Although Bull had the advantage of nearly a foot in height and almost fifty pounds, Hopkins stood toe-to-toe trading punches with the big man. Hopkins's shirt bulged tight as his muscles strained to land thundering fists against the bigger man. He was quicker than Bull by far and easily dodged most of Bull's blows. But all his strength didn't seem to even shake Bull back half a step.

Hopkins backed off, quickly grabbed his equalizer from the floor, and began swinging it furiously, landing blows that would have crippled or killed an ordinary man. One blow landed against Bull's shoulder, sticking the four-inch spike deep into his arm. Bull let out a wail of pain and pure anger.

Hopkins landed several more savage blows before Bull charged in close. Hopkins went for a headshot, driving the equalizer against Bull's skull with a sickening crunch. But the spike missed, and the equalizer splintered into pieces. The big man was dazed, and Hopkins stepped in to finish him off. He thundered the man with bone-jarring punches before finally hammering the big man to the floor.

Bull roared and jumped right back to his feet with unexpected agility. The two men wrestled around the entire room, scattering tables and chairs as they fought for the head hold that would break the other's neck. As they stumbled against the bar, Bull swung a high punch. When Hopkins raised his arm to block it, Bull slammed his forehead down almost on top of Hopkins' head with a sickening thud. The farmer grabbed at the countertop, almost collapsing as his wobbly legs refused to hold up his weight. Bull effortlessly lifted him up, flung him around in midair, and tossed him against the bar.

Pritchett watched the fight with amusement as Bull delivered the final punishment. The farmer howled in agony as Bull slammed a huge fist to his lower back. Again and again, Bull pounded all of his strength into his punches until Hopkins finally sagged to the floor. Bull tossed the barely conscious man against the wall and battered him senseless until Pritchett finally commanded him to stop.

"No, Bull! I don't want him killed. He'll be a good example for the rest of the squatters."

Pritchett looked around the room at the shattered furniture everywhere and at the bodies that were just now being carried out. The wounded were being fed whiskey for their troubles. He was glad now he'd found Bull stranded out in that desert.

Bull had offended someone in the worst possible way, though Pritchett never found out what the man had done. As punishment, he had been left tied down by stakes in the middle of the desert, miles from anywhere. Pritchett had rescued the man from the baking sun, and since then the man had shown undying loyalty to Pritchett.

Loyalty was very important to Pritchett. That's what bothered him about the new man, Jay. Pritchett had hired him because he thought he could be useful. After all, he was the only man who had ever beaten Bull, and yet he claimed he was just lucky. Pritchett thought otherwise.

The possibility was very real that Jay could beat Eddie Platt and Slade in a gunfight as well. Jay seemed so rebellious, so defiant. Pritchett couldn't predict how Jay would react under any given situation. That made Pritchett uncomfortable. He needed to always be in control of everything and everyone around him.

Pritchett walked to the door and took a deep breath. As he watched Peters and Cranston hurry toward the saloon, he thought about Jay again. Disobediently running the surveys according to his own rules, Jay was turning out to be a thorn in his side. One that might need to be removed. The survey teams had to be feared if they were to keep the farmers under control. Jay had single-handedly put an end to that by confronting Peters and his crew and sending them back to town.

Pritchett knew he needed to find some way to control Jay. There had to be something or someone important to him that Pritchett could squeeze. He shook his head again and stepped through the door. He was beginning to think he had made a mistake about hiring Jay. There was something about the man. He stopped and stuck his head back in the saloon.

"Take Hopkins home. But first, drag him up and down the streets so everyone can see him. Make sure they know what will happen if they refuse my terms."

Jay and Slade made quick work of the land surveys, and most of the day passed without incident. They rode to four small farms, all under a hundred acres, and were met at each with the same anger. Of course, they expected nothing less.

At the last farm, Mrs. Bennett, who worked her land with only her three sons, held the visitors off with a shotgun before a truce was finally agreed on. As soon as she had started to aim her shotgun, Slade's gun was up and pointed at her head. Jay raised an eyebrow at Slade's fast draw, then eased his horse out of the line of fire.

Another rifle appeared on the cabin's flat roof in front of a face that couldn't have been more than twelve years old. Jay's right gun came up in self-defense.

"We don't want to kill any children," Slade said quietly. The woman turned her head slightly and told her son to "get back inside," that she'd "handle this thing," but the young boy didn't move.

"You can't handle this alone, and you know your kid won't get a shot off in time." Slade paused. "We have a job to do, and we aren't leaving until we get it done. Dyin' won't serve you any purpose and I got no qualms about shootin' a woman."

Slade pulled back the hammer of his gun with his thumb, and its click rang out with dramatic effect in the silent evening.

"Nor I, about shootin' a kid with a gun pointed at me," Jay added, knowing his words were more threat than truth.

Jay watched and listened as he gazed over the bore sights of his gun, praying the boy on the roof wouldn't make any sudden moves, wondering if he would have time to decide whether or not to kill the boy if he moved. Mrs. Bennett hesitated, then licked her lip and glared at Jay, whose concentration was focused on her son. She began to lower her weapon.

"I tell you what," Slade said. "We're not here to cause any trouble. We'll leave our guns here. That way you'll have no need to worry." He eased the hammer back and dropped his gun into the dirt. "Go 'head, Jay."

Jay didn't move for a long time, his aim still on the boy. He glanced at Slade, his eyes silently questioning Slade's action. Slade nodded, and Jay looked at Mrs. Bennett. She nodded, then lowered her shotgun all the way.

Jay lowered his gun to his side, not at all comfortable about riding around a hostile farm unarmed. He looked at Slade again, then tossed both guns to the ground. Without another word, Slade led off and Jay followed, speaking after they were around the side of the house.

"That's pushing it a bit close," he said, looking back warily.

"Not really. The boy was scared to death, and she was already giving in."

"I can tell you don't have much experience with womenfolk," Jay said. "They've been known to change their minds on occasion, you know, most times without any good reason at all."

"That's true," Slade agreed, patting a small flap on the left side of his saddle pack. Jay guessed the flap concealed a spare gun.

The evening passed quickly, and dusk was falling as the men retrieved their guns and rode back toward Bronco. The Spencer farm and the Boykin farm surveys would take up most of the next day, so the two men agreed to meet at sunrise to continue their work. Jay bypassed town, heading instead for Winifred Evans's home. He suddenly felt a compelling need to see her, almost as if she were calling him.

It was long after dark when he pulled up next to her front door. Even as he rode over the nearest hill, he saw her standing in the doorway, her silhouette backlit by dull lamplight. He dismounted and ground-tied his horse.

"Bit late to be outside, isn't it?" Jay asked lightheartedly.

"I've been waiting for you."

"Doesn't surprise me," he said, leaning in for a light hug. "I had the feeling you were calling me, your voice a whisper on the night breeze."

"You read poetry?"

"Naw," he said with a chuckle. "I tried to read a poetry book one time, but I got bored with it real quick. I think I used it for fire kindling one night."

She laughed and turned into the cabin. Jay followed her inside and closed the door behind him. Two plates sat on the floor on opposite sides of the dim lamp, and a single potato sat on each plate.

"I don't have much to offer," she said.

"You have more to offer than most people," Jay replied. "And I'm grateful for all you give."

"Oh, my," she smiled. "Such charming manners."

"I got a quick lesson in manners today at the Hopkins farm." He gingerly fingered his scratched cheek. He tore hungrily into the dry potato, swallowing too much and choking on his first bite.

"Do you have water?" he asked hoarsely.

"Of course."

Miss Evans stood and reached behind her for a jug and two cups from a shelf. As she poured, Jay looked around her home. There was only one room, about ten feet square. There were shelves on the walls, which were otherwise bare.

A heavy sheepskin rug and pillow on the floor served as the bed by the stove and a folded blanket was neatly placed at the end of the rug. On hooks near the door, a heavy coat and two other well-worn dresses hung over a small pile of neatly folded clothes and other necessary items. Otherwise, the room-home was clean and uncluttered.

"Do you like it?" she asked, waving an arm around.

"Comfortable. I don't have as much."

Silence. Miss Evans reached for Jay's hand.

"You are troubled."

"Something about this whole surveying assignment just doesn't feel right. I have a lot of questions."

"Answers?"

"None yet." Jay took another bite of his baked potato. "But you know that."

"It's why you're here."

"Is that inside information?" Jay asked, nodding at the way she was holding his hand. "Or just straight thinking?"

"Both," she replied. "Twenty years ago, I was a slave on a plantation. But two years before, I had a vision that I knew showed me the opportunity and the way to freedom. I waited for it all those months, being patient while other runaways were caught and beaten, or worse. But my vision came true. It's not important how I knew. I just waited and it happened." She looked at Jay for a few seconds.

"When I see things, it's because they've happened already or will happen sometime in the future. I'm alive and free because I trusted my vision."

"And so I should trust you?"

"I know it's a lot to ask."

"It is."

"You're special, Jay. You face a challenge far greater than any you've ever faced. Let me help you."

Confused, Jay simply nodded, and she continued.

"What did you find today?"

"People, not squatters," Jay said, eating more potato. "People like you and me, with families and homes and farms and gardens." He paused to take a long drink of water. "I found people willing to die, or kill, to keep what they consider is rightfully theirs."

"Wouldn't you do the same?"

"Sure. But Pritchett's got the legal papers, and therefore he's legally in the right."

"And what bothers you about that?"

"These farmers really believe they have grounds to dispute Pritchett's claims. Most of them won't sell at any price. I talked to some of the farmers, and some of them are saying that Pritchett might be doing some illegal activities on the side. They don't seem like they're lying. I mean, they can't all be lying, can they?" Jay clenched a fist in frustration. "But Pritchett certainly has the law firmly on his side."

"There is a higher law than any man's," Miss Evans added.

"I'm just not sure I'm on the right side. I shouldn't even be involved at all. I should just be moving on."

"That's what you do best, isn't it?"

Jay just looked away.

"You met the woman."

Jay looked at Miss Evans and smiled.

"She's probably what started all these crazy thoughts I'm having. I started asking questions because of what she said, but I'm the only one asking questions. If I ride out, Pritchett wins. And if Pritchett wins, she and all the rest of the farmers lose.

"It's inevitable, anyway. There's no way they can stand up against Pritchett. Slade says he's got money and lawyers. He's got friends that are US Marshals, I hear. If I side with her and the farmers, I'll have to take my chances again with the law. And sooner or later, I'll have to face Slade—"

"He is not your enemy, Jay."

"You don't know him like I do. If there's one breed of character I know well, it's gunfighters."

Winifred Evans looked at Jay for a moment, then glanced away.

"You should trust me. I know these things."

Jay shrugged. Miss Evans nodded and changed the subject. "What about the woman?"

"Her name's Marabelle Hopkins." Jay smiled again. "She's beautiful. She's the one." He nodded. "Yes, ma'am. She's the one."

"I know she is your small island of happiness in a growing sea of trouble. But I'm not so sure she is the one for you."

"Well, I'm sure."

Winifred Evans gently pulled her hand from Jay's hand and looked away sadly.

Pritchett looked up as Slade walked casually into the saloon. He waved him over when Slade looked his way. He sat opposite Pritchett, placing his gun, Pritchett noted, closest to Eddie Platt. Platt seemed not to notice. The floor squeaked behind Pritchett as Bull shifted his weight.

"I pay you to make things go smooth," Pritchett said.

"You pay me to enforce your policies," Slade said. "Not to get involved in squabbles between your workers. Our job was to go out and survey farms, and we did just that. And we did it peacefully. That's Jay's job. Your words, Mr. Pritchett."

"Humph," Platt interjected. "Maybe I should go out with the next survey to keep Jay in line."

"And get killed," Slade said, verbally dismissing Platt from the conversation.

"You're sure about that?" Pritchett asked.

Slade nodded and took another sip of his watered-down whiskey. "I'm sure that Platt wouldn't stand a chance against

Jay. Sure, Jay said his guns weren't for hire, but that don't mean he isn't a gunfighter."

"You like him, don't you?"

"He's a likable kind of guy, Mr. Pritchett. He's respectable. Look," Slade continued. "Chuck Peters stepped out of line out there. He puffed his chest and tried to step over a grown man's pride in front of his family. Even a gun doesn't give a man the right to do that. Jay set him straight is all. And we got the job done peacefully."

"We?" Pritchett asked.

"Yes. You pay me to see that the job gets done, so I hung around to make sure it did."

Slade took a few minutes to tell Pritchett about his own solution to the Bennett problem and their success in completing the surveys at several of the smaller farms. Pritchett nodded but remained silent as Slade continued.

"You see, Jay's like me a bit. He's got a strong idea of right and wrong. Stay within his idea of right, and he'll work for you."

"And how far does your idea of right and wrong extend?"

Slade smiled. "Mine is probably more influenced by gold," he said with a chuckle. "But to answer your question, I won't shoot anyone who isn't shooting at me."

"And if some innocent people get hurt or killed?"

Pritchett looked Slade directly in the eye, knowing the man's next words would either make Slade his enemy or give him a free hand at whatever scare tactics he could dream up.

"What you do or what you tell your other hands to do is your own business. Just don't ask anything unreasonable of me."

That was the answer Pritchett wanted to hear, and he leaned back in his chair and smiled. He wanted to know that Slade's services were his exclusively, and he couldn't say that of Jay just yet.

"And if I tell you to take on Jay?"

"I think he's scared," snarled Platt.

"I reckon everyone's entitled to an opinion, no matter how

stupid it is." Slade looked right at Eddie Platt. "And yours is about as stupid as any I've ever heard."

Eddie Platt's eyes flared, and he started away from the table. He looked down at the last second to see Slade's gun pointed at him under the table, still in its holster. He froze and sat back down.

"Easy, Eddie." Pritchett reached out an arm to restrain Platt, not seeing that Slade had already restrained him. Pritchett looked at Slade.

"I see you're not afraid of Eddie." The laugh danced in Pritchett's eyes.

"Wouldn't cost you anything if I had to kill him," Slade smiled. "Jay will cost you a bit more, though."

"How much?" Pritchett asked. "Er, just in case, mind you."

"Five hundred."

"Five hundred! That's preposterous." Pritchett shoved himself away from the table. But he knew he'd pay.

"The risk is considerably greater where Jay is concerned. My odds of success are fifty-fifty," Slade said. "Then, there are the odds of coming away successful, but injured."

Slade paused a moment. "You should know by now, a gun-fighter's job takes only a few moments of time. A challenge, a bullet or maybe two, and then it's over. But that's not what you're paying for. You pay a gunfighter for the risk he takes, not for the individual job."

Pritchett leaned forward against the table with both hands palm down.

"Well, where is he now? He didn't come back to town with you."

"Don't know."

"Maybe he went to see that Witch Lady," offered Platt.

"Hmmm. Now there's a thought," mumbled Pritchett. "She seems to be important to him. Maybe you ought to pay her a visit, Eddie. Why don't you ride out there tomorrow. Tell her I'd like to see her."

"Be glad to, Boss."

Pritchett knew he could count on Eddie Platt for his less scrupulous errands. The man was good at that kind of stuff.

"Excuse my sayin' so," Slade spoke up. "But that might not be such a smart move."

"You don't know human nature like I do, Mr. Slade," Pritchett smiled. "I have a feeling Jay might be a bit more reasonable if he knew his actions might affect someone special to him."

"Or he might not," Slade added.

CHAPTER 8

S LADE DID NOT SHOW UP at the time and place he and Jay had agreed to meet. Jay waited until just after sunrise, then headed out to the Spencer farm alone. The ride out was long and boring, since the farm was over four hours away from town, so Jay had plenty of time to think.

The conflict between Pritchett and the squatters was far more than just a disagreement. It had the makings of war and, good guy or bad guy, nice or mean, Pritchett had the law on his side. Even if the homesteaders' accusations of underhanded activities by Pritchett could be proven, Pritchett was the sort of man who would resort to anything to keep from losing.

Although Jay did not trust Pritchett, he was not convinced his boss was doing anything illegal in his dealings with the homesteaders. Pritchett paid his wages, though, and would certainly expect loyalty. Jay knew his loyalty was already in doubt after he'd sent Peters and the others back to town. Yet someone had killed the Hopkins cattle as a message, and it was clear Pritchett was going to be blamed.

Was it possible that Pritchett could have court documents changed? Maps forged? Jay dismissed the idea. Pritchett might have one or two maps altered, but twenty-six? No, that would amount to a conspiracy.

Still, the Hopkins property wasn't at all like the map indicated. All the homesteaders he had met were families who had put down roots, not temporary intruders upon the land. And there was Marabelle. He had never known a woman so strong-willed and bold, so beautiful. Jay found these qualities very attractive.

This business of keeping the peace was becoming more than just a job. It was becoming personal. There was no way he was going to ride away from this, and he certainly wasn't going to side against Marabelle or her family.

With that realization, things all of a sudden got real complicated. If he didn't side against Marabelle, he'd have no choice except to side against Pritchett and his men. And Slade. Killing was about to erupt, and Jay knew he was going to get caught right in the middle.

Surveying the Spencer farm would be his last job for Pritchett, he decided as he rounded a small knobby hill leading to the farm. But maybe there was still a way he could fulfill his role of peacekeeper.

Suddenly, he reined his horse up, halted by the stench of charred wood and burned flesh. He reached for his Winchester. Jay dismounted to scout around, but all that remained of the homestead were charred ruins. The barn was completely destroyed, and the main house was nothing but a blackened, burned-out shell. Only one wall stood in its interior.

Jay walked slowly around to the rear of the house, holding his breath as he crept past the single wall. He saw feet and legs first. The body was not burned. As he walked closer, he saw that the man was dead, lying face down in a pool of dried blood. He had been shot twice in the back of the head. *Another statement,* Jay concluded. After all, it only took one bullet to the head to kill a man. Anything more was anger, hatred, or provocation.

The man lay near the body of a boy in his teens. The right side of the boy's head was nearly caved in, crusted over with dried blood.

Jay continued searching among the ruins of the house. He found two charred skeletons in a side room. Both were the remains of young children. If there was a mother, she had not been in the house when the murderers struck.

Jay hurried out of the shell of the house and leaned against his horse, feeling a mixture of anger and sorrow. His mind flooded with flashbacks of returning from the hunting trip ten years past, to find his own family dead in a burned-out cabin.

In the barn, Jay found the remains of several horses, but no human bodies. Jay was about to return to his horse when he noticed the wagon turned on its side to the right of the house. A hand lay in view just beyond the wagon. Jay went over to the wagon and saw the body of a woman.

She'd been stabbed four times, and her clothing was torn. But she didn't die without a fight. In one clenched fist, she held a handful of cloth. In the other hand, she held something silver. Jay pried open her fist and grabbed the large, silver medallion. Anger and hatred boiled inside him as he recognized Bull's medallion with the three diamond-shaped holes in it.

Jay knelt beside the Spencer woman. Hers had been a slow and agonizing death, and she'd suffered a beating and worse humiliation. Again, his thoughts drifted back to his own family, and a tear trickled slowly down his cheek.

Jay gently laid the woman aside and scanned the numerous tracks around the area. He soon found what he was searching for, the tracks of the horse with an abnormal front left shoe. He nodded to himself and tucked the medallion in his back pocket.

Jay had started to pick up the woman's body to carry it to where he would bury the family when he heard the sound of snapping wood. He spun around, gun instantly in hand, but no one was there. The sound could only have been made by something or someone moving, and there was only a single wall to hide behind. Jay approached the wall slowly.

Survivor or witness? Or had someone waited around? Just an animal?

He crouched, then lunged and rolled to the other side of the wall, gun cocked and ready, only to face a little red-haired boy about six years old. The boy wore only pajamas and was covered with dirt and soot. Jay eyed the boy for a moment, then put his gun away and walked toward him. He got to within a few paces of him before the boy backed away. Jay stopped and squatted, and the two looked at each other for a while.

The boy shook with fear and after a moment, Jay held out his arms as if asking for a hug. The boy looked at him for a while longer, then slowly walked forward. When he reached Jay, the boy hugged him with a grip tighter than any little boy should have. Jay held the trembling boy silently for a long time, then picked him up and carried him over to his horse. He sat the boy in the saddle and gave him a small piece of dried beef, which the boy tore into savagely.

Jay made a crude grave for the family and marked it with a cross fashioned from two small branches from a nearby bush. Then, he mounted up and headed to the northeast. It would take hours to get the boy to town, so Jay decided to take him to the next property he was to survey. He held the boy in front of him in the saddle with one hand while holding the reins to guide the horse with the other. The boy neither spoke nor cried.

They arrived at the Boykin homestead about an hour after dusk. Jay couldn't see details in the dark, but according to the map, the Boykin place was in the middle of a wide valley formed by two north-south hills. The house was well lit, and the aroma of food filled the air, but Jay rode in with his Winchester ready. He was taking no chances. He'd had enough surprises for one day.

Jay was just about to holler out when his horse whinnied and shied away from the bushes to his left. Instantly, Jay covered the shadows with his rifle.

"Sound off or you're dead," he said quietly.

There was no sound from the darkness, but Jay had learned long ago to trust his horse's reactions.

"Last chance. The next sound you'll hear will be a shot from this Winchester."

"Don't shoot." The timid voice belonged to a woman.

"Come out here in the light." She did as she was told. "Who are you?"

"Paulette Boykin. What do you want here?"

"Where's everyone?" Jay ignored her question.

"They went to town. But they're coming back soon," she warned.

"I've got a little boy here who needs help." Jay watched the slender figure move slowly toward him.

"Better bring him inside," she said.

Jay walked his horse behind the woman and dismounted at the front door. He reached up for the boy who again clung to his neck and wrapped his legs around his waist. Jay comforted him with soft words as he carried him into the house behind the woman.

In the soft lamplight that flooded the main room of the cabin, he saw she also carried a rifle. Jay looked around for anything out of the ordinary, but everything seemed normal. He was surprised to see that Paulette Boykin was only about fifteen years old. She was dressed in a long blue cotton dress, and her long brown hair was woven in a single braid that reached down to her waist.

Paulette knew the child as one of the Spencers, but she didn't remember his name. She tried to take him from Jay to clean him, but the boy wouldn't let go. Jay ended up cleaning the boy himself while Paulette fixed him a plate of food. Jay sat the boy in his lap at the table. He clung to Jay's arm with one hand and stuffed food into his mouth with the other.

After the boy had finished eating, he again clung to Jay as they followed Paulette back into the family room to wait for the rest of the Boykin family to return. By the time the wagon pulled up, the boy was asleep and still holding on tightly to Jay's neck.

Three people walked through the front door, each surprised to see a stranger sitting in their house, pointing a gun at them. The two elder people were large and heavyset, while their son was tall and lanky.

"Jason!" exclaimed Mrs. Boykin.

Jay flinched at the mention of his real name, then saw that the woman was concentrating on the little boy. The coincidence was unnerving.

"That be your horse out there?" asked Mr. Boykin.

"Yes. My name's Jay."

"You the one who works for Pritchett, aren't you?"

"I'm not so sure of that now."

"Well, either you do or you don't. Which is it?"

"And do you have to point that gun at us in our own house?" Mrs. Boykin added.

"Sorry, I was just being careful," Jay said as he holstered his gun. "This boy's family was murdered over yonder. I brought him here since you're the closest folks around. I was hoping you could take care of him for a while."

Jay explained what he'd found at the Spencers' farm, omitting who he thought was responsible. Then he explained what he'd found at the Hopkins's place. When he finished, Mr. Boykin told Jay of their earlier encounter with Pritchett in town, and how the man threatened them to either give up their land for a price or die.

"And he says he's got legal papers too."

"He does," Jay added. "I've seen 'em, and I carry a copy of the maps and writs of land assessment for my land surveys. But for the transaction to be legal, he has to buy you out at a fair price. That way, if he's ever taken to court, no one can claim the sale was forced, not if the sale is fairly priced."

Jay knew there wasn't much use in completing the surveys, since he now had no doubt the man was using murder and threats of violence to coerce the farmers into selling their farms and houses. Yet so far Pritchett had been very clever to remain hidden behind the law. No doubt, his hands were clean while others had done his dirty work.

Jay's decision was clear. He would help the homesteaders. He had to, even if it put him on the wrong side of the law again. It was simply the right thing to do. There was no way he would stand around and do nothing while people were murdered or cheated out of their homes.

"And did you hear what he did to Harold?"

"Harold?" Jay asked, shrugging.

"Harold Hopkins," Mr. Boykin continued. Jay's eyebrow lifted. "Had that animal of his, Bull, beat the stuffing out of him. Almost killed him, he did. Then he dragged him around town for everyone to see. Said he wanted to teach us a lesson. You know he's behind these murders and Hopkins's ruined cattle and feed, don't you?"

"I have my suspicions. Bull killed Mrs. Spencer, I have no doubt about that, but I don't have any evidence for sure that Pritchett was involved."

He pulled out the silver medallion from his back pocket and told them where he'd found it. The medallion might not be enough to convict Bull in court and wouldn't even cast a whisper of guilt at Pritchett, but it was enough to convince Jay.

"Pritchett's got to be stopped," Jay said calmly.

"Oh? And who's going to stop him?" Boykin asked sarcastically.

"We have to draw the line at murder."

"We? And just who is the 'we' that's any match for Pritchett's gunmen, or his money?"

Jay knew he was the only man who had even half a chance against Pritchett. Even if Pritchett was responsible, he was too smart to get his own hands dirty. On the other hand, Jay had never seen Bull unless he was standing in Pritchett's shadow. It was likely that Pritchett was at the Spencers' place, right beside Bull as he murdered Mrs. Spencer and her family. Trying to prove it, though, would just be a waste of time.

Suddenly, he recalled Marabelle's intuition about the farmers' claims. According to Pritchett and the Bronco land office, none of the homesteaders had filed claims on county land they occupied. Pritchett's legal basis rested on that fact, and on the legitimate maps and writs he had obtained.

The whole issue seemed to center around whether or not the legal documents Pritchett possessed were real or fake. If they were forgeries, then Pritchett could be made to answer to federal law. The only way to be sure was to find the original documents in the Regional Land Depository in Abilene. The trip there and back would take about two weeks, so Jay decided to leave first thing in the morning.

"If you don't mind, I'll bed down in your barn. I'll be leaving for Bronco at first light to return some lost jewelry to a man called Bull."

"Bronco?" Mr. Boykin asked. "You serious? Bull's always with Pritchett. And he's got two gunfighters and half a dozen other men protecting him. You're just going to ride in there and take them all on?" Boykin harrumphed and leaned back in his chair. "Well, it hasn't exactly been a pleasure knowing you, but I have a feeling we won't be seeing you alive again."

"Maybe," Jay answered. "But Pritchett doesn't know that I know he murdered the Spencers. I'm still one of his workers, so I'll be able to get close to him."

"And then what?"

Jay had no answer for that question yet. He couldn't just kill the man on a hunch. And he had a feeling Pritchett wouldn't be easily scared off.

"Well, good luck to you."

Jay knew he'd need more than luck. He'd have to get to Pritchett without Slade around. Otherwise, his quest for justice might end before it began.

Slade realized he was taking a huge risk, trying to help the old woman. Lord knows he didn't owe Jay any favors, but like he told Pritchett, there was a limit to how much he could allow the line between right and wrong to be bent. He could not condone taking hostages. If something were going to happen between Jay and Pritchett—and that seemed inevitable now—he saw no reason why an innocent woman should be hurt or killed in the cross fire.

The only question unanswered for Slade was whether or not he would be involved in the quarrel. That question would be answered when Pritchett paid, or refused to pay, his fee of $500.

He was able to keep an eye on Eddie Platt all day since Pritchett had assigned them to survey farms northwest of Bronco. Just before dark, he rode out of Bronco to the south a few minutes after Eddie Platt and his motley crew left for the Witch Lady's shack. His roundabout route was longer than Platt's direct ride, but he pushed his horse hard and arrived at her shack just as the sky was darkening.

"You've got to come with me now," he said simply. "You're in danger."

She nodded knowingly. "It's Mr. Pritchett's men, isn't it?"

"That's right." Slade reached out a hand and lifted her up onto his horse behind him. They raced up the nearest hill, barely cresting the top as Platt and his men rode up the valley.

From there they watched, hidden in the scrub grass atop a hill 200 yards away, as Platt tore down the woman's home and burned it in frustration at finding no one home. Slade knew Eddie Platt was a renegade. Even Pritchett's influence wouldn't have prevented Platt from delivering the Witch Lady dead, or nearly so.

The closest homestead was the Hopkins farm. Midnight was nearing as Slade let her down at the front gate of the Hopkins farm and disappeared back into the darkness.

CHAPTER 9

J AY RODE INTO BRONCO JUST before noon on Wednesday
and headed straight for the saloon. He had learned that
Pritchett conducted all of his business there, his only office
in town. Where Jay found Pritchett, he knew he would also find
Bull. Jay tied his horse at the hitching post in front of the saloon
and decided on a hunch to check the front left shoe of Bull's big
roan, a chestnut sprinkled with gray. Its shoe was normal, so
he checked the other horses nearby until he found the horse he
was looking for.

The beige dun had a half-inch hole in its front left shoe.
Before he talked with Bull he would find the owner of this horse.
He was rising up from examining the horse's hoof when Chuck
Peters and Eddie Platt emerged from the saloon laughing. They
froze the instant they saw Jay at the horses.

"Hey! What the hell are you doing? Stealing our horses?"

Jay ignored Platt's baited question. "Who owns this horse?"
he demanded.

"That's Mr. Pritchett's horse," Peters said. "What of it?"

"I found tracks from this horse out at the Hopkins farm. I
figure your boss was out there burning their grain and crippling
their cattle a couple of days ago. And he was at the Spencer farm
when that family was murdered. So now I aim to have a talk
with him about all that business. Where is he?"

Eddie Platt stepped to almost within arm's reach of Jay. "I

told you before, you got something to say to Mr. Pritchett, you got to go through me first."

Jay jumped around the hitching rail as Platt went for his right gun. He grabbed the man's wrist, locking the gun in its holster, and knocked his left hand away as Platt went for his other gun. Jay drew his own gun and arched it up high, catching Platt across his face. Platt fell unconscious to the boardwalk.

Peters took off running up the boardwalk, dodging awkwardly between the passersby as he fled. Jay trotted after him, slowing to a walk only when he saw Slade step out of the boardinghouse. Slade walked toward him, and they faced each other in front of the open doorway of the general store.

"I'm looking for Pritchett and Bull."

"I don't know that I can help you there."

"You can't, or you don't want to?"

Slade said nothing for a few seconds. "What's your interest?"

"They're murderers." Jay reached into his back pocket and handed Bull's medallion to Slade. "I found this out at the Spencer farm. Mrs. Spencer had it clutched in her hand as she died. They brutalized her before killing her, her husband, and their three children. Pritchett's horse's tracks were all over the place and at the Hopkins farm as well."

"Come on, Jay. What does that prove? Mr. Pritchett has at least half a dozen horses, and he'll ride any one of them on any given day, in no particular order. He always loans out his spare horses to his riders."

"So how do you explain that?" Jay pointed to the medallion Slade held.

"Seems obvious to me that Bull needs to answer for his crimes. But a horse track won't convince a judge that Pritchett was involved."

"I don't need to convince a judge."

"You can't prove it, Jay. What are you going to do, take the law into your own hands and bump heads with Pritchett?"

"Someone has to. He can't go around killing people without answering for it."

"Well," Slade said, shifting his hat. "If I can give you some advice—"

"I don't know if I can trust your advice any longer, Slade."

"My word's as good now as before," Slade said tersely, eyes narrowing.

"Maybe."

"I told you, don't challenge me again. You take that back, or make your play, mister."

Jay simply looked at the man, then started to turn away. Slade's eyes flared, and he reached out and grabbed Jay's arm. Jay twisted around, easily breaking Slade's grip, and shoved the man back against the wall near the general store's open door. Both men knew this was the moment of truth.

They were poised to draw their guns when two elderly women stepped through the door right in front of Slade, both chatting freely. Neither woman realized the danger they had walked into.

Jay and Slade froze, eyes on each other and the women. Both waited for the other to make the move, neither wanting to be the one responsible for the accidental shooting of innocent women.

Suddenly, one of the women dropped her bag of foodstuffs, prolonging the interruption. With the heat of the moment past, Jay turned and walked back up the street to the saloon to get his horse.

Bull and Pritchett would have to wait. Guns wouldn't solve this problem, Jay knew. What he needed was proof, hard evidence. He mounted up and rode back toward the store. Slade had just finished helping the woman with her bag. Slade stepped warily near the edge of the boardwalk as Jay spoke.

"What I meant was, since we're on opposite sides now, it's not too smart us advising or confiding in each other."

Slade nodded, accepting the apology.

"You sure this is what you want to do?"

"It's what I have to do."

"Same applies to me."

"He's payin' you to kill me." It was not a question. The unspoken had finally been said.

"He hasn't put up my price, yet."

Jay nodded, figuring as much. He started to turn away, but Slade spoke again.

"But if he does pay, you and I will talk."

Jay nodded. "Face to face, I hope."

"No other way for respectable men to talk, I reckon."

Jay tipped his hat and rode away, more than slightly bewildered. He wouldn't have believed he would ever back down or apologize to any man. Even still, he knew he had insulted Slade needlessly.

"I thought that was going to be it," Pritchett said as he walked up behind Slade.

"Almost was. Time wasn't right, and neither of us really wanted it." Slade turned and looked at his employer. "He's smart, Mr. Pritchett. He'll choose the time and place if he can. I'll tell you something else too. I've had this nagging thought about who he really is. Now I'm sure."

"What?"

"I thought he was familiar first time I laid eyes on him. Ever hear talk of a brown-skinned gunfighter, a legend of sorts, out west? A man called Jason Peares?"

Pritchett stood dumbfounded, staring at Slade as if hadn't quite heard him. "Jason Peares?" he said finally. "The outlaw? I heard he disappeared out in California a few years ago."

"I heard the same, but it fits. He was a wanted man up until about five years ago. Had a price on his head as high as $5,000, I heard. Maybe ten. Two-pistol, half-breed gunfighter, half-Black, half-White. You heard the Witch Lady call him Jason a couple days ago when he almost shot those kids."

"I'll be damned," Pritchett said. "I'll raise your fee to a $1,000."

Slade raised an eyebrow. "Two thousand—"

Pritchett started to protest.

"—in gold."

Pritchett relented. "Agreed." The two men shook hands.

CHAPTER 10

MARABELLE SAT ON HER FRONT porch watching Daniel and Mr. Boykin fix the rear axle on their wagon. A lot had happened in the week following Jay's mysterious disappearance. Rumors were plentiful, but none of them made any sense.

Some said Jay had been killed and buried in the hills out east of town, while others said he'd just been run out of town by Pritchett's gunfighters. Marabelle knew in her heart Jay wasn't one to be scared off, and she prayed he hadn't been killed.

But what had become of him?

She thought about the farmers' plight. Everything they owned was tied up in their land and their crops. Everyone knew Pritchett was only legally bound to give them the cash value of their land and equipment assets, minus the common sense decrease in equipment value due to age. Though he claimed he would offer top dollar for the homesteads, all the farmers knew he wouldn't have to account for the potential value of their crops. If the farmers sold or were forced out, they wouldn't have enough resources to start over somewhere else. All the years of hard work would have been for nothing.

The farmers knew the only way they could stand against Pritchett's tyranny was to combine their strength. They were betting all their lives on their unity. All the small farm families had moved onto the large farms, and the families formed groups that circulated throughout the county, tending to all the farms.

Their strategy was clear. Pritchett would need a small army to run them all away.

Today one person from each family would be traveling to the next closest town of Bresley since Pritchett had cut off all credit in Bronco. Seven wagons would carry them out and back, loaded down with supplies. Bresley was forty miles southwest of Bronco, and it would take the small caravan almost two days each way to make the trip. Marabelle was making the trip for her family.

She fidgeted with her hands as she thought about Jay. He wouldn't leave her mind, not even when she slept. Now she felt an ache in the middle of her chest, an ache that could be healed only by the answer to one simple question.

Where is he?

She spent every waking moment thinking about him. She tried to deny her own feelings, but she couldn't lie to herself. She was in love. Her eyes clouded with tears at the thought.

A hand touched Marabelle's shoulder, and she looked up into green eyes.

"May I sit with you?" Miss Evans asked.

Marabelle nodded, wiping her cheek with the back of her hand.

"Don't despair," the woman said. "Jay has not abandoned us."

Miss Evans had been staying with them for a few days. They'd found her sleeping on their porch the morning after Pritchett's men brought Hopkins back from town. She didn't say why she had come, but they soon found she was a happy person to have around, and they needed another worker around the farm with Harold Hopkins laid up.

The doctor had said he was lucky to be alive. He had several broken ribs, internal bleeding, and a skinned up back from being dragged through the streets of Bronco.

"His face might be scarred," the doctor said. "Especially around the eyes, and he will certainly be puffy for a long time. With a month of bed rest and no hard work, he'll recover just fine. Might not smile as well, though, with two lost teeth," the doctor joked.

Nobody laughed.

At first, Miss Evans tried to sneak away, knowing she was a heavy burden to the family. Daniel rode out and caught her afoot barely a mile from the farm. He threatened her with bodily harm if she was going to let the whole county think that the Hopkins family would turn away a neighbor in need of help. Miss Evans simply smiled and got on Daniel's horse. Since then, she had done more than her share of work.

Witch or not, Marabelle thought, *we aren't going to leave her without a home.*

As if reading her mind, Miss Evans spoke up. "You don't need to be afraid of me," she said. "I'm not really a witch like everyone thinks. I'm just a woman, like you, you know. Just a bit older and wiser."

"People say things."

"I know. They just don't understand," she said. "People are afraid of what they don't understand. He understands me. Says I have a gift. That's all."

"What kind of gift?"

"Sometimes I know things." Miss Evans continued to lead the conversation where Marabelle needed it to go. "Like I know how he feels about you."

She patted Marabelle on the arm and nodded when the young lady's eyes brightened.

"He loves you, you know."

"That's crazy," Marabelle said, but she blushed anyway. "We only talked for an hour."

"You love him, don't you?"

"Well, I don't know—"

"Come now, child," Miss Evans said, chuckling. "An hour was enough for him to know how he feels about you."

"You don't know that for sure," Marabelle argued.

"Why, of course I do," Miss Evans said and laughed. "He told me!"

Jay took six days to reach Abilene. He thought about many things during that time, but mostly about Marabelle. He regretted not telling her where he was going. But he couldn't risk Pritchett finding out by accident or otherwise.

And what about me and Marabelle? Could I stop running from the past? Maybe hang up my guns and live like a normal man? Stop drifting? Settle down with a wife and have children? Work a farm?

Beyond the fantasy and the dreams, there was the current reality.

What is Pritchett after? What is big, dark, and deadly that Miss Evans spoke of during our second meeting? What would Pritchett do now that I'm gone? What will he do when I ride into town with legal evidence?

Then Slade crossed his mind. Jay had apologized to him because the man was reasonable and because Miss Evans had said Slade was not his enemy. What if she really was right about the man? She'd asked for his blind trust, and he'd given it. Were it not for her, either he or Slade would be dead right now. Of that, Jay was certain.

He rode into Abilene early Tuesday morning on the seventh day of his trip and went straight to the land office, next door to the office of court records. The office was huge. There were eight large rooms filled with so many cabinets there was hardly space between each row for a man to squeeze between them and open the drawers.

After hours of researching and crosschecking maps and property book lists, Jay had located maps of all twenty-six of the homesteading farmers around Bronco. The clerk told him to take the maps to the front office to have copies written. Jay handed them to the senior clerk and was told to pick up his copies in three days and the cost would be a dollar for each map.

"Why so much?" Jay wondered.

"You ain't payin' for the maps, sonny," the old man replied. "You're payin' for our integrity, our accuracy, and our authenticity."

"How's that?"

"We got us a special license to make copies. And all copies have to be signed by a judge."

"How would the judge know whether he was signing fakes or not?" Jay asked. He was getting close to the critical information he needed.

"Lad, lad," the old man said, obviously bored with simple, common knowledge. "We use special codes we keep locked back there. That signature code tells the judge the copy is legal and all. Only we and the judge know the code, and we change that code every time we get ourselves a new judge."

"I see," Jay mumbled. "So if someone wants a map faked, he'd have to get one of your staff to fake it so the judge would sign it."

"And, that person gets ten to twenty years hard labor if he gets caught. Somethin' goin' on here I need to know about, sonny?"

"Hold on a minute."

Jay went out to his horse and retrieved Pritchett's roll of maps, then went back into the land office.

"Can you tell me who wrote these copies?"

"Sure," the old man nodded as he examined the map of the Hopkins farm. "See this code here?"

Jay nodded as the man pointed to a seven-digit number in the upper right corner.

"What does it mean?"

"Well, now, if I told you that, you could swindle a pile o' gold by makin' maps. Hold on while I go check the book."

The man returned five minutes later with a suspicious look in his eyes.

"What's goin' on here, lad?"

"Can I talk to the man who wrote them?"

"He's dead."

Jay nodded. "How'd it happen?"

"'Bout two months ago, he was shot down in the street, right out there. Nobody knows who did it or why. Except maybe you know, eh?"

"Yeah," Jay mumbled. "But I can't prove a thing."

That was becoming a phrase too often used where Pritchett was concerned. It wasn't hard to imagine the man bribing a land office clerk with more money than he'd otherwise see in a hundred years, then killing the man after the maps were delivered. He'd save a lot of money that way, and also eliminate a loose end. But Jay still didn't know why Pritchett was so desperate to get the land.

"Any chance I can get those copies first thing tomorrow?"

"It'll cost you. I'll have to work through the night."

"I'll pay two dollars for each map," Jay said.

"I was thinking more like three."

"Two."

"Well, you could wait three days like everyone else."

"Two dollars apiece," Jay said, his clear brown eyes burning into the old man's.

"Look, I got a wife and six kids—"

"I'm not interested in your family problems, mister. I want the maps in the morning, and I'll pay two dollars apiece."

The clerk started to speak, but froze at the cold, hard look in Jay's eyes.

"Er...in advance?"

Jay counted out fifty-two dollars—part from Pritchett's advance for his first week of work and part from money earned from Cassie's cattle run—and held the money out over the table. The man grabbed it, but Jay didn't let go.

"First thing in the morning," Jay reminded him, letting go of the money. "And signed."

The old man nodded, and Jay turned to leave. He stopped at the door. "Don't even think about being late, mister," Jay added without turning back.

With that, Jay left the office. He crossed the street and walked down to send a wire message to Bronco.

Pritchett is smart, Jay thought. *Real smart.* He smiled to himself. Maybe a bluff might work.

A farmer burst into the saloon without warning, shotgun aimed and ready. The sudden intrusion interrupted Slade and Pritchett's quiet conversation. Pritchett had barely sucked in his breath in surprise when Slade reacted, drawing his gun and shooting before properly having his sight fixed on the intruder. The farmer didn't even have time pull his trigger before Slade's shot slammed him back out the swinging double door.

Pritchett leaned back in his chair, nodding graciously in Slade's direction. Then he angled his head toward the sheriff.

"Drag that piece of trash back where he came from," he said. "And bring me another drink, Barkeep. And one for Mr. Slade too. Anything he wants. Even the good stuff."

"Yes, sir. Right away, Mr. Pritchett!"

"Bull couldn't have done that," Pritchett said as two men walked out the doors to drag the man away.

"Not likely," Slade agreed.

The dead man was the last of the small independent farmers in the far northeast part of the county. The rest had either been killed or burned or had packed up their belongings and abandoned their property. Some had joined with the larger farms, under the umbrella of protection offered by the resurrected Bronco Farming Cooperative.

The time for compromising with the farmers was past. Now, Pritchett had to figure out how to handle the co-op. Previously, he'd known of the co-op as just an informal gathering of farmers aiming for marketing power with the regional produce buyers for the big cities. He never figured on the co-op becoming a defensive network that actually protected its members.

He had more men coming out from Tucson, but they wouldn't

arrive for another few days. With Jay away for a while, Pritchett had sent Bull and Peters to round up the new men. Besides, he still had Slade to take care of any problems he might encounter. Until his army arrived, the farmers could enjoy their small victory. At least things were going a bit more smoothly now that Jay was out of the picture.

Pritchett had given up wondering where Jay had gone or whether he was coming back. There was always the possibility he had been scared off, but Pritchett found that extremely unlikely. Jay was probably off somewhere devising a plan. Of that, Pritchett was sure. Maybe he was rounding up his own army, maybe a band of his former outlaw friends. As if to punctuate his thoughts, Paul Cranston stormed into the room.

"Mr. Pritchett, I think you better see this!"

Pritchett took the piece of paper with scribbled printing on it, then immediately sat up straight in his chair.

"Damn. That's one smart son-of-a-gun. Looks like I underestimated him again."

He passed the message over to Slade.

HAVE COPIES OF ORIGINAL MAPS AND PROOF THAT YOU MURDERED FEDERAL LAND OFFICE CLERK. STOP

WILL ARRIVE WITH RANGERS IN SIX DAYS. STOP

BE GONE OR MEET JUSTICE. STOP

JAY.

"So that's where he's been," Slade said.

"I'd better disappear for a while. There'll be Texas Rangers, Federal Marshals, and every other two-bit lawman in the territory riding into town after me in less than a week."

"Hank Shrider'll be here by then," Cranston offered. "That's eighteen men."

"Against Texas Rangers?" Pritchett shook his head. "No, I wanted to confine my little war to Bronco, not get in a shooting war with the law. They'll hang around for a while, but they can't stay forever. They'll go back home, then we'll come back."

"Maybe he's bluffing," Cranston said.

"How do you figure?"

"Well, he's only been gone a week. Took us four days just to get those other maps wrote. I figure there ain't no way he can make the whole trip in less than sixteen, seventeen days total."

"You just might be right, Mr. Cranston."

Pritchett saw Cranston's eyebrow raise a bit. After all, he never called anyone "mister" unless he wanted to bestow some amount of importance on that person. The more important his men thought they were, the more eager they were to let him use them.

"Come to think of it, maybe he doesn't have the maps at all," Cranston added.

"Not quite," Pritchett said, watching Cranston's ego deflate. "He's got the maps, otherwise he wouldn't know about the dead clerk. Yes, he knows, and he's real smart too. Smart enough to—"

"No." Cranston snapped a finger suddenly. "He ain't got the maps. Not yet! He's bluffing you. He figured everything out maybe, but ain't got the maps wrote yet!"

"Yes," Pritchett nodded slowly. "His rangers won't be here in six days. He's just tryin' to spook us. It'll take them nine days for sure, but not six." Pritchett rubbed his chin thoughtfully. "That means we've got three days to get somebody to Abilene to stop Jay from getting the maps and the evidence. If we can get to him before he leaves town with the rangers."

"Off hand," Slade said, "I'd say that isn't possible, not in three days."

"But it is," Cranston countered. Pritchett looked at him.

"Well?"

"I have a friend in Abilene. I could send him a wire."

"You know, Mr. Cranston," Pritchett leaned back in his chair again, "I could use another foreman to go along with my new bodyguard."

Paul Cranston smiled. Pritchett glanced from Slade to Cranston and back again. He had regained control of the war.

Jay thought about visiting the US Marshal as he rode through Abilene and past his office. But without proof of any wrongdoing, neither the marshal nor the rangers would consider intervening in one small town's problems.

If Pritchett fell for the bluff, he might panic and figure Jay was bringing back the law for him. On the other hand, Pritchett had proved himself very imaginative and resourceful. He wouldn't quit and run even if he did believe the rangers might show up. He would fight back somehow.

But how? Ambush? Certainly not against highly trained Texas Rangers. Pritchett isn't stupid.

Yet if Pritchett didn't fall for the bluff and didn't believe the rangers or marshals were coming for him, then ambushing Jay by himself was no problem. Jay decided to take a roundabout route home.

But what if Pritchett has contacts in Abilene, Jay thought suddenly.

Certainly, Pritchett now knew Jay's location, and just because Jay was more than six days' ride away from him didn't mean he was out of reach. A hired gun could be following him, so he'd have to watch his back all the way.

Jay frowned at all the possibilities. *Am I just driving myself crazy? Overestimating my opponent? No, I have to trust my instincts.*

He recalled Miss Evans's words. *"You face a far greater challenge than any you have ever faced."*

He knew that challenge was Pritchett. It would take fast guns and faster thinking to take the man off his fence post.

Jay picked up his maps at eight o'clock sharp the next morning and headed out of town. He rode quickly down a side street with a lot of shops. When he saw the bright yellow-and-black-stripe silk dress hanging up in the fabric store window, he knew immediately he'd pay any price for it. To see Marabelle with her beautiful dark brown skin in a real silk dress was too perfect an opportunity to pass by.

He ground-tied his horse and pushed at the door. It wouldn't open, but he could see almost a dozen people inside through the front window. He tried it again, then a woman walking by snickered and said it was the only door in town that opened outward.

Jay thanked the woman, then pulled the door open and went inside. He paid almost ten dollars for the dress and had it boxed and wrapped. He had just stepped outside and closed the door behind him when he heard someone call his name from the street.

Jay looked up to see four men riding up the middle of the street. One of the men was already pointing his gun. Jay spun to his left and drew his right gun. The first man's bullet slammed into the wall where Jay had stood barely half a second before, then Jay regained his balance and fired one shot at the lead rider. He knew without looking he had scored, but he had to get out of there fast. He cradled the gift in his left arm while he holstered his gun, spinning and lunging for the dress shop door.

Just as quickly, he forgot it opened outward and slammed headfirst into the heavy door. He bounced off as three more bullets thudded into the wood by his head. Jay groaned and reached up for the doorknob, this time pulling it open. He slammed it behind him and raced straight for the back door with both hands wrapped around his package. Behind him, he heard loud cursing as the three men tried to get the front door open.

Jay made it through the back door and took off running around the end of the block of stores. He made it around the corner before the first of the men raced into the alley. He raced up the boardwalk and mounted his horse on the run. As he passed his followers' ground-tied horses, he grabbed their reins and led them off. He would be safe from pursuit, at least for a while.

He'd been lucky, that's all, and he'd underestimated Pritchett again. Jay was angry, cursing his own carelessness. Against a man as dangerous as Pritchett, he couldn't afford to be sloppy.

He couldn't leave any detail unconsidered, no matter how small or insignificant. He'd better keep his mind on the trail and on business, and not on Marabelle, or he'd likely end up dead.

He left the extra horses far out beyond the edge of town and stopped to tie Marabelle's gift behind his saddle.

Pritchett slammed a fist to the table after reading the wire. The men in Abilene had missed Jay and suffered one dead and one injured.

"Dammit! Four men can't even handle one man!" Pritchett yelled. "One man, all by his self!"

"Not when that man is Jason Peares," Slade said quietly.

"Did you say Jason Peares?" Cranston stared at Slade in disbelief.

"I did."

Cranston stood slowly. "Nobody said nothin' about takin' on Jason Peares. I'm sorry, Mr. Pritchett. You'll have to find another foreman."

"You scared?" Pritchett prodded, more than a little irritated.

"Damn straight! You should be too. Hell, I'm riding out of here right this minute!"

Pritchett's eyes flared at the man's insubordination, but he calmed himself quickly as Paul Cranston ran out the front door. The man was a coward anyway. He ought to have the deserter killed as a message to others, but he had more important issues to deal with now.

That Jason Peares has got the whole town scared, he thought. *He can't be that good.*

Pritchett slammed his chair backward, angry at letting the man rattle him. Then he realized the man didn't bother him as much as his reputation. *The legend.*

He took a deep breath to steady himself, then walked calmly to the door. He stopped and turned to face Slade.

"Well, Mr. Slade. I've paid you. Can I count on you to fulfill our agreement?"

Slade smiled and patted the newly acquired sack of gold hanging from his belt. "Of course, Mr. Pritchett. It pains me that you even have to ask."

CHAPTER II

J
AY RODE INTO THE BUSTLING town of Bresley only five days after leaving Abilene. One more long day in the saddle and he'd be back home, facing a confrontation he wasn't anxious for.

For now, he was free and enjoying the uneventful ride across the plains with the sun on his back and the clean, slow breeze in his face. There'd be time to face the war later.

He should've bypassed the little town, but he was running low on ammunition and other supplies. Jay rode up and down the town's two streets until he found the general store. He made his purchases and looked around for somewhere to eat. Across the street, there was a small kitchen house next to the hotel. He walked his horse across the street, wrapped the reins loosely around a post, and stepped up onto the boardwalk. Then, he heard the voice.

He'd been thinking about Marabelle all morning, but the coincidence of her being in that particular town was something he had not imagined. She burst out of the sewing shop with an armload of fabric rolls. Gasping, she stopped so suddenly the two women following close behind her piled into her and all three ladies stumbled forward.

Marabelle dropped her fabric and untangled herself from the others, then took a halting step forward. Emotions battled across her face as she decided what to do next. Jay simply gazed at her from across the street, his heart thumping wildly in his chest. For a moment, he stood there unable to move.

Marabelle quickly stepped off the boardwalk and ran across the street. She literally jumped into his arms with a tight hug that lasted for nearly a minute. Then, she leaned back and kissed him hard on the mouth.

"I thought I'd never see you again," she said.

"I knew I'd see you again," he returned. He took her face in both hands and caressed her cheek, then he kissed her. "I have something for you."

He pulled her over to his horse, untied the box, and handed it to her. Her eyes beamed with joy as she tore the box open. She was more than grateful as she squelched a scream of pleasure. Looking even lovelier than he had imagined, she spun around with the dress held up in front of her so everyone in her group could see. Finally, she settled down.

"Everyone seems to know we're in love except us. The Witch Lady—" She hesitated. "I mean, Miss Evans told me...."

"I can't wait to hear what she said. Why don't we help the rest of your group get loaded up?" He nodded toward the group of Bronco farmers he recognized behind Marabelle, who were packing supplies into two uncovered wagons.

"Sure. Why don't you help them?" She pointed up the street where more farmers were loading up five more wagons. "Then on the way back, you can tell me where you've been." She punched him playfully on the arm. "I thought you'd left me."

Marabelle turned and walked back to the wagons, cradling her new dress. Jay watched her for a moment, then led his horse up the street to the warehouse for feed and farm supplies. Two hours later, the heavily laden wagon train crawled slowly back toward Bronco County. Marabelle rode alongside Jay, out in front, as he patrolled for Pritchett's men with his Winchester at the ready. The land was mostly flat, so no one could sneak up on them or mount any kind of ambush.

Marabelle told Jay about the revival of the Bronco Farming Cooperative. All the remaining farmers had combined their credit and buying power to purchase enough supplies from Bresley, since Pritchett was making things difficult in Bronco. Even though some of the smaller farms had been burned-out, the co-op easily absorbed the losses.

The farmers had organized themselves into four groups besides Marabelle's group. Two of the groups rotated through all the farms in the county, tending and harvesting the crops. The other two groups were armed bands of men and women who provided protection for the farmers.

Pritchett's men had tried many methods to isolate the farmers, but the co-op always prevailed. Leaving only enough men and women to guard the two or three large homesteads where all of the farm families now lived, the rest of the people traveled from farm to farm, most days working with a hoe in one hand and a rifle in the other.

Pritchett had called for more gunmen to harass the farmers, but rumors circulated that he still couldn't deal with the co-op. But there were no second chances, and Pritchett and the farmers both knew if the farmers didn't get their crop to the market, they were all ruined. The farmers were fighting for their lives now and had shown Pritchett that the united farmers were indeed a formidable force.

Pritchett knew his only chance at defeating the co-op now was by preventing the farmers from getting their crops sold at the regional markets that were, in most cases, several days' ride away. He abandoned most of his hit-and-run raids. Instead, he had his men concentrate on finding and destroying the farmers' harvest storage areas. He succeeded for all of one day.

The farmers adapted quickly by pooling all of their horses and wagons together, creating a mobile harvest and storage wagon train that they drove directly to the markets from the fields. Pritchett's response to this new strategy was to have his raiding parties ambush the wagon trains along their routes. There were many routes, though, and Pritchett's manpower was stretched too thin. Many times, his raiders attacked the wagon trains only to be confronted and beaten back by a fierce mob of armed farmers that outnumbered and outgunned the raiders.

He also sent his raiders to the farms to attack the farmers while they worked, but again the groups of armed farmers protecting the workers thwarted Pritchett's strategy. Despite heavy losses, he stuck to his plan. He knew if he could take out even half of the harvest, the farmers would be ruined, and he would win.

Marabelle saved the worst of the news for last. Though only one farmer had been killed in the week before she and her group left for Bresley, the co-op's resources were almost stretched to the breaking point. They were losing too much of their harvest. Pritchett was winning. And the farmers knew he had enough money to keep buying more gunmen.

"The real solution to the problem is to get rid of Pritchett," Jay said that evening after dinner. They had eaten with the rest of the group, then moved off to make their own private fire. They both needed private time—to be together, just the two of them. Time to talk about anything or nothing at all.

"How?" Marabelle asked. "How do we get rid of him?"

"I don't know yet. He needs your land for something that's very important to him. Otherwise, he wouldn't waste his money and men trying to possess it. He's not just land hungry. This has to be so big that he's willing to risk tangling with the law, willing to risk murder."

"But why? What's so important that he'd kill all the farmers?"

Jay shrugged. "Grazing land?"

Marabelle shook her head. "None of the cattle trails to New Mexico or the Indian Territories come anywhere near here."

"Minerals?"

"No one's ever found so much as a pebble of silver or gold."

"Water rights? I hear water for irrigation of large farm projects can start some lengthy and expensive legal battles. If someone owned all the water rights—"

"Only the farmers would be interested in that, and we get enough to water our crops from rainwater."

Jay pondered her words for a moment. "But what if someone was planning a large farming operation in the near future? A huge farm much larger than all of yours put together. Maybe Pritchett's trying to monopolize the farming market in this area. They'd need additional water."

Again Marabelle shook her head. "There aren't any rivers for miles. And only four or five creeks about the size of the one bordering our land. That's hardly worth fighting about."

"Underground water?"

"I doubt it. We have to drill down almost fifty feet just to find well water for the house. And sometimes that dries up, and we have to dig another well. There's just not enough water underground to fight about."

"Railroad?"

"Where from?" Marabelle asked. "Where to?"

"Then what?" Jay asked. "What's so important to kill over?" Marabelle just shrugged.

"And Miss Evans said it's big, dark, and deadly. Was she giving a real physical description or just describing some kind of abstract image in her mind that maybe represents something else?"

Jay toyed with the fire, then continued. "Whatever it is, it's crucial to Pritchett's plans. He knows what the farmers need, and he's prepared to do anything to hold those needs ransom. The only way we're going to defeat him is to find out what he needs. Only then will we have equal power over him. Without that knowledge, we're at his mercy. He'll continue to wear us down."

Marabelle nodded and started to say something but fell silent for several minutes. Jay waited for her to put her thoughts in order. Her next question came suddenly.

"Do you like children?" she said.

"I suppose I could," Jay said awkwardly. "I've never been married, so I don't have any of my own. I don't really have much experience in that area, although I've become attached to the Spencer kid. Seems we share some things in common." Jay stared at the fire for a moment, then added, "I think Jeremiah and I could get along too."

"There's something I've been wanting to tell you." She hesitated. "About my son." She paused again. "About his father."

Jay sensed Marabelle was uncomfortable, so he avoided looking at her. Instead, he picked up his twig and poked at the fire again.

"We never got married," she said. Quickly, she added, "But we would have. He died before Jeremiah was born. He got sick."

"You don't have to explain," Jay said.

"You have to know. Before we get real serious."

"Too late for that."

She turned to face him suddenly, shocked.

"I mean," he blurted out. "It's too late because we're already real serious." He smiled and took her hand in his. "Whatever happened in your past has made you the woman you are today. And that's the woman I love. The rest doesn't matter."

"Yes, it does. My son is a bastard child because I didn't get married before...." Her voice cracked a bit.

Jay nodded and squeezed her hand tighter. He wanted to tell her it was okay, that it didn't matter, but in a rare moment of true clarity, he realized her confession was very important to her. He didn't want to just brush away her concern as a trivial issue.

"Maybe he won't always have to be."

"All right, gentlemen. It's time for a new strategy."

Pritchett paced around the two tables where his eight men sat. In addition to Slade, Chuck Peters, and Eddie Platt, the newcomer Hank Shrider and his four men waited for Pritchett to outline his plan.

"I've tried every way I know to convince these farmers to move. I've offered to buy them out with very generous values for their land, I've threatened them, and I've cut off their credit. Hell, I've even killed some of them, but still they stay."

"This farming co-op has you beat," Shrider observed. He reached into his black vest and pulled out a rolled smoke, which he stuck between his thick lips. He struck a match with his fingernail and lit the cigarette.

Pritchett stopped pacing and eyed the man. "Mr. Shrider, you underestimate my commitment. I've tried to avoid slaughtering these stupid dirt throwers, but they don't seem to know any better. I've given them every opportunity to leave, so now I'm afraid I'm left with no alternative. My clients will arrive in three days with tens of thousands of head of cattle. The farmers must be gone in three days, one way or another."

He continued his pacing. "Mr. Peters, recall all your men from their patrols. Meet up with Mr. Shrider's men and ride out to meet our clients. Then bring in the merchandise from the west." He paused. "A lot of money is at stake here, gentlemen. I don't want any mistakes, and I don't want anything to happen to my merchandise."

The men sat watching Pritchett for a moment longer.

"That's all, gentlemen. You have work to do, so let's get to it."

Jay and Marabelle rode together most of the trip. On the last day, they decided to separate from the group and ride out to the Boykin farm to visit little Jason Spencer. When Marabelle asked him why the boy was special to him and what they had in common, Jay grew quiet. Then he began talking, slowly opening up the wounds of the past.

He told her where he was from, beginning with the tragic death of his family and how he felt bonded with little Jason. He talked about his outlaw days and the years after that, of drifting and finding odd jobs on cattle drives and ranches.

"Reminds me of my brother," Marabelle said with uncharacteristic sadness.

"Oh? How's that?"

A gunshot in the distance interrupted them, and they turned to see a lone rider coming up the trail in the distance. He glanced across the grassy plains toward the wagon train they had left. The wagons were pulling into a cluster about a mile away.

"Let's go," Jay said, spurring his horse into a run. They arrived at the wagons just as the rider pulled up.

"We won," the rider said excitedly. Jay recognized him as one of the Bronco County farmers. "We beat 'em."

The rider related the recent events and how Pritchett and his men were seen leaving town earlier the same day.

"Every last one of them," the rider concluded.

"Well, maybe now we can get back to our own homes and farms," Marabelle said.

Jay was skeptical. "You're saying they all just rode out. No explanations?"

"Most of them left yesterday. But Pritchett and three or four others rode out this morning. Anyhow, it's over, and we won!"

Jay watched the rider and wagon drivers whoop up the noise and start the group moving again. He and Marabelle were left breathing their dust.

"What's the matter? You heard him. It's over."

"Something's not right about this," Jay said thoughtfully. They spurred their horses into motion, heading again to the west. "I sent Pritchett a wire last week that said I had proof of his crimes and hinted I was coming back with lawmen beside me. He responded by having some men in Abilene jump me. That wasn't enough to get him to leave Bronco, but now all of a sudden he just rides out? There's something wrong here."

"Maybe he ran out of men or money or something," she suggested.

"Pritchett's not a quitter. If the law doesn't scare him, then something bigger is in the works. Part of his plan. What I can't figure out is why some of his men left yesterday and Pritchett just left this morning."

Jay thought for a while, then shrugged. "I guess we'll just

have to wait until we get back to town to find out. But you were saying something about your brother. Something I said reminded you of him."

"He left home ten years ago because he didn't think much of farm life. Wanted to live the trail life and ride the range." A confused look came over Jay's face, but Marabelle didn't seem to notice.

"But Daniel would only have been nine years old. Didn't he say he hadn't been out of this part of Texas?"

"No, not Daniel. I'm talking about Sam. He went—"

Jay pulled violently on his reins, and the horse reared back on its hind legs and hopped to the side. The name from the past exploded in his ears. He suddenly felt like he was choking, unable to breathe. He was hot, feverish, and freezing cold at the same time.

"Sweet Jesus," he muttered over and over again, eyes clamped shut. He felt a hand grabbing his arm.

"Jay, what's the matter with you?"

He looked over at her for a moment. Then he lifted his face to the sky.

"Jay, what's wrong?"

He looked at her finally.

"I killed Sam Hopkins."

CHAPTER 12

"**N**O, HE WAS SHOT BY an outlaw—"

"Marabelle, my given name is Jason Peares."

Marabelle tried several times to speak, but no words came from her mouth. Instead, she spurred her horse into a walk. Jay rode silently for a long time before speaking.

"He was my friend, or so I thought. We spent a few months together riding the range. We rode herd together and worked the horse ranches too. We hunted, fought, ate together." Jay looked over at Marabelle. "Then one day, Sam pulled a gun on me in front of the sheriff's office. He said he was only studying me, looking for my weaknesses so he could turn me in for the bounty." When he told one of the deputies who I was, the deputy panicked and drew on me. I pulled my gun too, and then everybody was shooting.

"Sam took one of my bullets in the chest. He was hurt bad. I stayed with him, and he died in my arms.

"I ran for a while, but I couldn't handle the guilt and pain of killing my best friend. At least, I thought he was my friend. That's one of the reasons why I turned myself in and was tried in Santa Fe."

He paused for a moment. "That's why Daniel looked so familiar to me. I couldn't figure it out, but he looks just like Sam did six years ago."

The rest of the trip passed in silence, both wrestling with their own thoughts. They rode up the gently sloping hill that formed the eastern border of the Boykin farm, but they were more than a mile south of the main house. As they rode along the crest of the hill, Jay could see the entire expanse of the farm. There were no fences except for the small corral.

Another hill formed a natural western border. The farm stretched for another mile to the south before bending to the west, cradled between the hills. The half-mile-wide valley was stock full of crops of all kinds, ready to be harvested. Jay could see several wagons and maybe a dozen farmers working the field.

Despite his gloomy mood, Jay noted the day was as beautiful as any he had seen. Then a frown creased his facial features. The rumbling sound he had thought was thunder was becoming louder.

Almost at the same time, Marabelle called his attention to the darkening storm cloud on the horizon behind them. He squinted his eyes against the shimmering heat waves that danced along the land. Suddenly, he realized with a twinge of panic that what he thought was a storm cloud was actually a dust cloud rising over the hilltop around the bend in the hills. The cloud and the noise were far closer than he thought.

In a flash of intuition, Jay realized what Pritchett's ultimate objective was. Miss Evans had said it was big, dark, and deadly.

A stampede!

Even as the thought tumbled through his brain, a black sea of animals rounded the turn of the hills. The low rumble, no longer muffled by the hills, suddenly erupted into a roar. Jay looked back toward the Boykin house, but already some of the workers who were close to their mounts had jumped on their horses or mules and raced out of the valley death trap. There were too few animals to ride out and the wagons could never be turned in time. The rest of the workers simply ran for their lives.

Jay saw Mrs. Boykin hobble out from around the front of the house and head for the eastern hill with little Jason in her arms, but she couldn't run. He knew she would never reach safety in time. Jay shouted for Marabelle to stay where she was, then spurred his horse down the hill. He kept low to the animal's neck to reduce wind drag and raced up beside Mrs. Boykin. He jumped down and helped her onto the horse and threw little Jason up in front of her. Then, he smacked the animal hard on the rump and ran as fast as he could.

The noise was deafening. He stumbled as the ground vibrated beneath his feet. He scrambled up the hillside as the first cattle of the herd raced past beneath him. But a glance to the side told him he was not safe. As the stampede bowed outward around the house, some of the cattle spilled up the hillside toward him.

Jay was instantly enveloped in a dust cloud so thick he couldn't see his hands or the ground as he clawed his way up the hill on all fours. He couldn't get air. He was choking. Every breath he sucked in rasped noisily in his throat as he breathed in dust and dirt. He couldn't hold his breath, and he couldn't cover his mouth with a kerchief because he needed both hands in his scramble for survival. His heart pounded, and his lungs felt like they were going to explode. One steer passed above him, barely an arm's reach away, and another raked its hoof across his back.

He fell to the ground from the impact, but somehow he scratched his way back to his feet and continued to climb upward. His ears hurt, his head throbbed, and his throat was raw. Then suddenly, he felt hands grabbing him, pulling him upward, and he was safe.

Jay collapsed, coughing and gagging as he tried to breathe. Several of the farmers pulled him to safety and backed away to give him room to breathe. After a few minutes, he was able to clear the dust out of his throat and drink water from a canteen Marabelle handed him. He gazed into her eyes, those beautiful brown eyes now so full of love and sadness.

The stampede lasted an impossibly long two hours, and when the dust finally settled there was nothing left of the homestead. The field of crops was completely plowed under and only a few sticks of debris remained of the house. Next to him, Mr. Boykin comforted his sobbing wife. Paulette tried to calm a hysterical

little Jason as other farmers stared down into the valley in disbelief.

"It ain't right, Jay," Mr. Boykin said. "That thievin' bastard
planned to downright murder every one of us, women and children too. I hate to admit that we're beaten, but it's time to cut
our losses and quit this fight. We're damned lucky we didn't lose
everybody down there."

"I'm inclined to agree with you," Jay said, looking down into
the valley. "We can always start over somewhere else, but only if
we're alive to do so."

Boykin nodded. "Besides, by the time those cattle get through
running all over yonder, there won't be anything left for anyone
to farm."

Jay nodded. "Our first responsibility is to get word to the
other farmers. We've got to get everyone out of the county. Did
you folks get enough crops to the market to cover expenses and
last the winter?"

Mr. Boykin shook his head. "Not even close. We got about
half as much as we needed. We were banking heavily on the
Palmer and Johnson crop 'cause their farm is almost as large
as all the rest of the farms combined. Pritchett probably knows
that too. They're right out in the middle of open range. If they get
caught in front of a stampede that size, there'll be nowhere for
them to run."

"Let's get these people started to the Hopkins farm," Jay suggested. "That's the closest place."

"Right," Boykin agreed. "Pritchett won't run the stampede
there because it's abandoned and has been harvested already.
It's going to be a long walk, though. Any horses that didn't get
trampled down there," he pointed into the valley, "are probably
scattered from here to California by now."

"Sooner we get started, sooner we get there. But we ought to
send word to the others," Jay said.

Boykin nodded. "We moved all the farm families to the Palmer
and Johnson farm for safety last week, after the supply group
left for Bresley. There are other groups like ours all over the

county, tending to the harvest. By the time all the farming teams get rounded up and back to the Palmer and Johnson farm, it'll be dark. No way they'll be able to pack up and move everyone out at night."

Jay scratched his head. "I'm worried about them too. Looks like we'll have to spend the night at the Hopkins farm. Then all the other farmers can come and get us, and we'll ride out of the county together in the morning."

"It's going to be a long night for them folks." Mr. Boykin nodded toward the valley again. "That must've been close to 10,000 head of cattle down there. Maybe even more."

Another farmer Jay hadn't met added, "How in the world did they organize that many animals and get 'em runnin' in one direction? Pritchett must have one hell of a support crew ridin' for him. Take close to a hundred men, maybe more if he cares about rounding up strays that cut loose of the main herd."

"A hundred men," Boykin mused. "Another reason to quit this county. If they run that stampede at night, there's no way to stop it."

Jay pondered this for a moment. "There's only one way I know of to stop a stampede."

Jay outlined his plan, and Mr. Boykin sent his son ahead to the big farm with the details.

CHAPTER 13

Pritchett sat on horseback on a rolling hill a few miles northeast of the huge Palmer and Johnson farm. He could hear Chuck Peters fidgeting next to him. He stared into the darkness, seeing nothing, but anticipating the sweet victory of the coming disaster. In a few minutes, he would win the war. With nearly all the farmers living together on one farm, this was his opportunity to wipe out his enemy. Decisively and completely. Best of all, the stampede would leave very little, if any, evidence behind.

He wished he'd thought of this strategy earlier. Even still, the victory would be his in mere minutes. In his imagination, he could already hear the screams of the helpless farmers as the three-pronged cattle stampede crashed through the ranch house after sweeping across the expansive farm. No one would be spared death, not even those gathered in the massive house. There were simply too many of the animals. The families who lived in tents beside the house certainly had no chance at all. There would be no crop left to harvest and no one left to cry about it.

Pritchett glanced sideways at Peters. In the pale moonlight, he could see the man was shaking.

"Don't think of this as murder, Mr. Peters. Just think of it as total victory. Our enemy is down there, and tonight they will die. We've given them more than enough warnings and plenty of opportunities to sell out and benefit from the inevitable. But they were all too stubborn and for that, they'll all die this morning. And we will soon become very, very rich."

Peters grunted his agreement as his horse skittered sideways.

"This is it," Pritchett said as his horse stepped nervously to the side.

Almost immediately, he was aware of a low rumbling sound, like faraway thunder. Within a minute, the sound was an earth-rumbling cacophony of charging, panicked cattle. He watched the lights of the ranch house brighten as the occupants awoke to greet their deaths.

"What's that?" Peters said, pointing off to the far left.

Pritchett raised himself higher in his saddle, standing in his stirrups. He witnessed the impossible.

The second oldest Johnson son, eighteen-year-old Michael, rode slowly along his assigned path two miles west of the big ranch house. The sky brightened slowly in the distance, and he knew sunrise was barely an hour away. His four-hour shift was almost over.

He didn't fully understand why they had to leave the farm. Something about Pritchett running 10,000 head of cattle across some farms. Michael found that hard to believe. He'd never seen more than a few hundred head in one place at one time. He knew the larger outfits could run a couple thousand head on a trail, but he couldn't even imagine 10,000.

His father and the other adults believed it. All the wagons were loaded down with as much supplies as they could carry, and all the farmers and their families were ready to ride out at first light. Michael's shift was the last group of lookouts to keep watch before the evacuation at sunrise. They were scattered around the huge farm, but he couldn't understand what all the panic was about. Nothing had happened all night. He'd been riding lookout for almost four hours, and he was hungry.

His stomach growled savagely, and he stuffed a fist over a jaw-breaking yawn.

Ten miles due south of Michael, Daniel Hopkins also had the early morning watch. He felt something was wrong before he heard or saw anything, but he couldn't make sense of the feeling. All was silent in the early morning darkness, but that was exactly what bothered him. There wasn't much in the way of critters in the desert-like country outside the farm, but he knew he should have heard at least the insects. Instead, there was nothing but total silence.

His horse shifted under him, muscles twitching. On edge now, Daniel pulled his rifle from its scabbard and peered into the darkness around him. He could see nothing in the blackness, but he still couldn't shake the feeling that something or someone was creeping up on him. He decided not to wait. He could always apologize later for a false alarm if that's what this turned out to be. He raised his rifle above his head and fired off three quick warning shots.

Michael's head bobbed forward twice before he was snatched from his fitful nap. At first, he didn't realize what he was hearing. Then gradually, the sound that woke him became a deep rumbling, and within a minute he could feel the ground tremble beneath his horse. His horse jumped sideways, then danced around almost in a circle before Michael got the reins under control. With the sudden movement, he had lost his bearing. Where was the ranch house? Where was the stampede? The sound seemed to come from all around him.

Peering into the darkness, Michael hesitated for a moment, but still he saw nothing. Fear and panic twisted his gut, and he didn't know what to do, which way to go. The sound of running animals was loud now. He reached for his rifle, then caught a flicker of movement to his left. He turned to find the source of the movement and was surprised that the herd was close, much closer than it sounded.

In a moment of clarity, Michael got control of his fear. He reached into his front shirt pocket for a short-fused stick of dynamite and remembered the plan quickly as he reached to his belt to strike a match. The first explosion would warn the ranch house. He would light and toss the other sticks with longer fuses on the run. The explosions would scatter the lead animals, turning the charge away from the farm. Michael struck the match.

A prairie squirrel, distracted from its race for safety by the sudden flare of the match, jumped and ran right between the horse's front legs. The horse, already jittery, reared on its hind legs and jumped to the side. With his concentration solely on lighting the fuse, Michael was tossed from his saddle. As he hit the ground on his rump, he saw the dynamite land only a few feet away, the fuse burning quickly to the explosive.

His eyes widened in panic, and he jumped up and lunged away, smartly putting his horse between himself and death. The stick exploded a second later. Though his horse absorbed most of the blast, Michael was still knocked off his feet. The hapless animal was nearly broken in two by the explosion, but fate sided against Michael as the dead animal landed across his legs.

He sucked in great gulps of air as he struggled to free himself from the heavy corpse. Even as he struggled, he fantasized that there was still a glimmer of a chance to survive. He pulled his legs free and grabbed another stick of dynamite and a match from the saddle pack, then took off running. He could only pray he didn't break a leg in a gopher hole.

Daniel lit his dynamite sticks and tossed them behind him on the run, knowing the fuses would burn for many seconds. He almost missed the first haystack in the darkness and had to turn back hard as his side vision caught the waving white flag marking the location of the hay pile. He tossed a match into the stack, staying only long enough to see it catch and burn, then raced across the farm to the next haystack marker.

Ahead and to his left and right, more burning haystacks lit up the horizon. It was then Daniel realized the real danger, the real desperation of their situation. Multiple fires meant Pritchett was stampeding cattle at them from several directions at once, not just one, as the farmers had figured he would.

Michael stretched his stride to his limit. He could see the lights of the house barely half a mile away. All he needed was three or four more minutes. He held onto the stick of dynamite until the last possible moment, then fumbled to light it on the run. He thrashed the match against his belt, and it lighted on the first try. Then he moved the flame to the end of the fuse.

The cactus tree appeared out of the darkness too late to avoid. Michael careened into the tree, screaming more in frustration than pain as the spiny thorns ripped away most of the left side of his clothing and skin. He spun a complete circle from the impact but managed to stay on his feet.

He continued to run without missing a stride. The unlit stick of dynamite was lost somewhere behind him in the darkness.

A pair of bucking horns appeared beside him and passed on his right, and he knew at any second he would be run down from behind. Another animal raced up on his left and he leaped onto the animal's back, clinging to its long hair in desperation. Then, the thundering chaos was all around him.

The steer under him bucked wildly and dipped its head in midstride, dancing left and right. Unbearable pain ripped through Michael's right leg as his steer crashed into another animal next to it. Then something hard and sharp hooked his left thigh and half-dragged him off the steer's back.

Michael, hanging off the side of the animal, grabbed a handful of the animal's coarse hair in his right hand. But he was too heavy. He fell under the barrage of hooves.

Pritchett watched dumbfounded as tiny flares of light flashed into existence, framing the homestead compound and dotting the distant fields. Suddenly the flares blossomed into huge bonfires that ringed the compound. Farther out in the night, explosions erupted over the din of the stampede, and more fires lined the boundaries of the distant farmland.

"Dynamite," Pritchett said quietly. "They're turning the stampede with dynamite and fires."

He waited for the ranch house lights to dim as the dust from the stampede obscured the structure, but it was not to be. Instead, the fires glowed eerily through the massive dust cloud. Soon the dust cloud and the sound from the stampede began to die out as the animals were turned away.

Pritchett swore silently to himself as he watched the fires light up the night all around the land below him. The farmers had outsmarted him. It was still too dark to see the results of his attack, but it was clear he'd be lucky if the stampedes even damaged a small fraction of the farmland.

Pritchett had been so sure of total victory. Now, with failure staring him in the face, he was forced to reconsider his situation. He'd counted on the remote possibility of having to deal with a few survivors, witnesses. He'd prepared a fallback plan to tie up those loose ends, of course, but his contingency had not counted on the entire band of farmers surviving his attack. And he knew human nature. The farmers would come back strong. They'd be mad as hell and even more difficult to defeat.

And somehow, Pritchett knew Jason Peares would be leading the counterattack against him. He turned his horse and headed back toward Bronco to prepare for the inevitable encounter. He smiled to himself in the darkness. He still had one more ace card up his sleeve.

CHAPTER 14

J AY LED THE CARAVAN OF farmers to the expansive Palmer and Johnson homestead. He nodded wordlessly at the four armed farmers that welcomed them through the front gate shortly after noon. Jay resituated himself in the saddle, trying not to slide forward and squash little Jason Spencer into the saddle horn.

The boy had attached himself to Jay shortly after they'd left the destroyed Boykin farm. Since then, he'd gone everywhere Jay went, even to the outhouse. Jay retrieved the reins from his young companion as they approached the main house. Marabelle rode beside him, and he reached for her hand as they rode up to the gathering of farmers in front of the main house. They still had not spoken their thoughts since the day before.

The main group of farmers had sent horses and two wagons to the Hopkins farm just after sunrise with the news that they had survived the night. The main group had not arrived with a wagon train to leave the county, and now Jay understood why. He scanned the collection of wagons that were being unloaded. As he dismounted, Paul Johnson, half owner of the farm with Steven Palmer, strode up angrily and confirmed his observations.

"We ain't leavin'." The man was tall, over six and a half feet, and was a shade or two darker brown than Jay. About fifty, he had short, curly gray hair. Jay knew of him to be a friendly sort, but now he looked downright mad, and he focused his anger right at Jay with a pointing finger.

"You hear me? I said, we ain't leavin'."

Before Jay could reply, Johnson turned away and walked over to his wife, who stood on the fringes of the gathering staring out at the barren land to the west. As Jay reached up for little Jason, Jay noticed Hopkins walking slowly toward him. He felt a sudden pang of anxiety and looked around for Marabelle, but she had already dismounted to greet her son with hugs and kisses.

Palmer, the other half owner of the big farm, joined Hopkins with Jay. He was as tall as Johnson, but was much stockier, in a lumberjack kind of way, with flaming red hair.

"What's with Johnson?" Jay said.

"They lost their son this morning. Michael."

"Damn."

"We took a vote this morning, Jay," Hopkins said. "We figure we can burn hay every night if we have to keep the stampede away. We have enough people to guard the farm in shifts, like you planned, every night. And we have enough people to harvest during the day. They trampled a small portion in the far north corner of the farm, but we got plenty left to get to the markets."

"Are you sure? More people might get killed."

Palmer nodded. "It was a unanimous vote. We figure there's sixty-five able-bodied men, women, and children who can shoot straight and work the fields. Pritchett's only got a couple dozen men to harass us. The rest will be tending his herd. We can send for some lawmen today. We'll have marshals here in a few days."

Jay nodded, wanting to change the subject. "You and I need to talk, Mr. Hopkins," Jay said, cradling little Jason against his hip. The boy held on with one arm around Jay's neck.

"I know." Hopkins looked away uncomfortably. "Look, I know this ain't gonna make it no better, but don't blame her for what happened."

Jay stared at Hopkins confused. "What? Blame who?"

"My wife was the only one there. Daniel and I were out in the field—"

"I thought you weren't supposed to be working yet." Jay could see the cloth bandage wraps bulging under his shirt.

"If I hadn't been, maybe I could've stopped them."

"Stopped who? What are you talking about?"

"They took her. Just rode in and took her. I'm sorry, but—"

"Took who?" Jay looked around anxiously. "Miss Evans?" She was nowhere to be seen.

Hopkins nodded. "I'm awful sorry. If I had been there, then maybe—"

"You might be dead. You couldn't have stopped them."

Jay knew Pritchett wouldn't have taken Miss Evans without a specific purpose. Everything the man did was part of a larger plan. He'd use Miss Evans to get to him, but Jay could only guess how exactly.

He started to share his thoughts with Hopkins but realized something was tugging at his pant leg. He looked down to see Jeremiah beaming up at him. Jay leaned down and put little Jason down beside Jeremiah, then ruffled both of their heads.

"What're you doing down here, little buddy?"

"Can I ride with you too, Jay?"

"Sure, you boys can ride with me anytime." He smiled at them. "But only if you give me some hugs." He pulled them toward him and heard Jeremiah giggling against his neck. When he pulled them away, he saw that little Jason was smiling for the first time. He patted them both on the cheek as Marabelle walked over to him.

"Can you take the boys for a minute? I have to talk to your pa."

Jay was just about to guide the boys over to her when he heard a shout from the front gate. He twisted around in his squat and saw the two riders approaching. Chuck Peters waved a stick with a white kerchief tied to the tip. The other rider was Eddie Platt. Jay knew Pritchett had sent Peters to talk, but he instinctively knew Eddie Platt's purpose had nothing to do with words. He turned back and smiled at the boys.

"Jeremiah, I want you and Jason to go into the house, okay? I might have to shoot my gun again, and I don't want you to get scared."

Jeremiah's eyes widened. He grabbed little Jason by the hand and nearly dragged him away. Jay watched the boys run into the house. He stood and checked his guns.

Peters pulled up in front of Jay. "I came with a message from Pritchett. For you, Jason Peares."

"I reckon I know what the message is," Jay said, keeping his gaze on Eddie Platt and his hands hovering over his gun butts. "Why don't you save me some huntin' time and just tell me where Miss Evans is."

Peters looked around at the farmers with a smug look on his face. "If you're talking about the Witch Lady, you don't understand. Mr. Pritchett—"

Eddie Platt interrupted. "Why don't we just spare the words?" He smiled and looked from Peters to Jay. "I didn't come here to talk."

Jay nodded, a cold look of understanding in his eyes. "I figured as much. But if you didn't come here to talk, then you came here to die."

The smile faded from Eddie Platt's eyes. He went for his gun.

Jay started to draw but flinched when an explosion of sound erupted from his left. Eddie Platt was ripped out of his saddle as if by a giant hand. Jay glanced to his left and saw Mrs. Johnson click back the second hammer on her double-barrel shotgun. She pointed the weapon at Chuck Peters. He raised his hands slowly.

"I just came to talk, ma'am."

"You killed my boy, mister. Why do I need to talk to you?"

Jay didn't let him answer. "Where is Miss Evans?"

Peters looked around at angry faces. He licked his lips, suddenly not so confident. He looked from Jay to Mrs. Johnson.

"I didn't have nothing to do with the stampede, ma'am. I just—"

"I'm asking you for the last time," Jay said. "Where is Miss Evans?"

"You're gonna kill me anyway, ain't you." It wasn't a question.

"You got one chance to live, Mr. Peters. Tell me what I want to know."

The man hesitated. "She's in the boardinghouse, in the last room at the back."

"Thank you. You go tell Pritchett I'm coming to get her at noon tomorrow. If he or any of his men are still in town, I'm shootin' to kill." Chuck Peters nodded but didn't move. Jason waved his hand like he was shooing away a stray dog. "You may leave now."

"Is she going to shoot me in the back?"

"I have no control over what she does. But the longer you sit there jawin', the more likely that outcome will come true."

Peters grabbed his reins and rode away fast. After a moment, Mrs. Johnson lowered the shotgun. Jay looked at her for a moment, then turned to face the farmers. He saw shock, surprise, and revulsion on their faces. Marabelle simply looked at the ground. Her mother seemed to understand what she was going through, as if sharing in her emotional turmoil. She wrapped her arm around Marabelle's shoulder.

Jay looked at Hopkins. "I wanted you to hear the truth from me first, not like this."

Hopkins stepped forward. "You're Jason Peares?" Jay nodded, and Hopkins grabbed him by the collar of his shirt with both hands, wincing with pain as he taxed his wrapped, bruised, and cracked ribs.

"You killed my son?" he whispered. Jay nodded again. "You murderin' son of a bitch!"

Suddenly, Hopkins released Jay's shirt and stepped back. "If it weren't for you...." He paused and closed his eyes. "If it weren't for you, a lot of good people would've died this morning.

But when this is over, we'll talk." He turned and bellowed to the farmers, "Let's have a meeting."

"Everybody inside," Palmer echoed.

Jay started to follow the group inside, but Miss Clara stopped him as he passed her and Marabelle.

"I don't reckon you'll be stayin' around when this is over?"

Jay glanced from Miss Clara to Marabelle, but she avoided his gaze. "I don't see how I can."

"Good." Miss Clara turned away and walked inside with Marabelle.

Jay was the last person inside the huge front room of the ranch house. A dozen conversations raged at once among the crowd of standing people, so he forced his way to the center of the room. He noticed that Palmer, Johnson, and Hopkins seemed to be the leaders that everyone listened to, so he stopped in front of them and held up his hands for silence.

"I have a plan," he said after everyone quieted down.

"Yeah," someone said from the edge of the room. "Ride in at noon and shoot everyone."

"Not exactly," Jay replied, looking around the room. "Pritchett is a thinker, a planner. He'll have two or three backup plans for everything we can think of."

"How do you know that?"

"He used to work for him, that's how."

"Maybe he still does. Maybe this is all part of Pritchett's trap. Maybe—"

Hopkins spoke up. "Now hold on a minute." He paused and narrowed his eyes at Jay for a moment, then pushed the obvious thoughts from his mind. "We'd all be dead right now if not for his quick thinking last night."

From the other side of the room, Marabelle added, "And he went to Abilene and brought back maps proving our claims on the land. I think we should listen to what he has to say."

Wisdom prevailed, and Jay related how Pritchett had responded to his bluff in Abilene, matching him move for move. He summarized how Pritchett's entire strategy was based on anticipating every possible reaction of the farmers and having contingencies to deal with all possibilities.

"What we haven't realized until now is that we've been playing right into his hands. We survived this morning, so he'll just put another part of his plan in place. That will continue until he finally kills all of us or forces us to leave."

"Your words sound reasonable," Palmer said, "but how do you know we didn't just beat him. He tried his stampede, and it failed. We can beat him at that every time now."

"And he knows that," Jay countered. "So he won't waste his time trying that again. While we're spending time and losing sleep waiting for it to happen again, he'll be preparing something else."

"How can you be so sure of that? What if you're wrong?"

"I'm not wrong," Jay looked at Hopkins. "He kidnapped Miss Evans."

"So?"

"He took her to control me."

"And?"

"He took her before the stampede just in case I survived the stampede. In his plans, he figured at least some of us would survive. He knew we'd either fight or run." Jay paused. "He knows I'd never run. He knows I'd go after him. He wants me to, that's why he took Miss Evans."

"You're saying he's using her to lure you into town so he can kill you?"

Jay nodded.

Marabelle stepped through the crowd. "So you gave him exactly what he expects. You told Chuck Peters you're riding in tomorrow at noon." She smiled as he nodded. "And you're hoping Pritchett will build his plan and backup options around your noon arrival."

"Except, I'm not going in there at noon, but at first light."

"No," Hopkins said. "If he's as smart as you're saying, then he's going to expect that, or at least plan for it."

"I'm counting on it," Jay replied. "Except Pritchett is going to be reacting to our plan this time."

"Plan?" Hopkins said warily. "What plan?"

"Ladies and gentlemen," Jay said slowly. "I think we ought to go into the cattle business."

CHAPTER 15

MISS EVANS LAY AWAKE IN the predawn darkness contemplating her situation. During her captivity, she had been given one measly meal each day. Though this was more than she usually ate before the Hopkins's generosity, she was sure Pritchett thought he was making life difficult for her. She was also allowed to bathe in private every third day. But she had company in the boarding room.

No one had figured out how she'd escaped Eddie Platt before, and she refused to tell them, despite threats of beatings. The beatings never came, but Pritchett took no chances. The guard's name was Hank, and his chair creaked as he shifted his weight to get more comfortable. He sat within arm's reach of the door. Miss Evans watched the sky brighten and decided to take her chance.

She'd been in custody for almost a week now. "Insurance," Pritchett said. Jay wouldn't be foolish enough to do anything that would endanger her life. Yet that was why she had to escape. She knew Jay would come for her no matter what his personal cost or how many guns he faced. She slid silently out of bed and crept toward the door. Her hand had just closed around the doorknob as Hank took a deep breath.

"Don't go and do nothin' crazy now, ma'am," he said sleepily. "I don't want to hurt you, and you don't want me to. If you get away this time, I get shot. We don't want that to happen, now do we?"

The man shifted his hat over his eyes and resettled in his chair. For a moment, Miss Evans considered making a dash for safety, but abandoned the thought just as quickly, knowing she didn't have a prayer of a chance to outrun the man. Sadly, she went back to her bed and lay down, facing the window. A tear fell from her eye as she realized she was leading Jay into a trap.

Jay sat near the early morning firepit and sipped warm coffee as he watched the sky brighten around him. *How will I get into town unnoticed? How will I find Miss Evans and keep her safe? What if Chuck Peters lied as part of Pritchett's plan? What if they moved her? Pritchett knows I'm coming for him. How many men are waiting for me? Would he be fooled and expect me at noon?*

For the farmers' part of the plan—that of stealing Pritchett's cattle—to be successful, Jay was counting on most of Pritchett's men initially being deployed in town as part of the plan to kill Jay. By all estimates, Pritchett could only have thirty men at most in town or working the herd, not a hundred like the farmers had thought after the first stampede.

After all, it took far fewer men to start a stampede than it did to actually control a huge herd. Pritchett wouldn't worry about rounding up strays. He could always hire more men to do that later, once the farmers were all dead.

However, if most of Pritchett's men were in town waiting for Jay, then the herd must be relatively unguarded. The only location near town where Pritchett could graze such a large herd and protect them with minimal manpower was the valley where Miss Evans lived. That was the farmers' destination. If the farmers had been successful with their part of the plan, then Pritchett would have been forced to redeploy his men to recapture the herd and deal with the farmers.

Their objective was simple. Armed with guns and dynamite, the farmers were to approach the valley over the western hilltops. Then, they would frighten the herd with carefully placed dynamite blasts to force a stampede that would scatter the animals all over the open plains.

The cattle theft had been scheduled for sundown last night. Jay had given the farmers strict instructions not to try to capture any of the men guarding the herd. He needed at least one of the men to report back to Pritchett for more men to help start the roundup. The herd was important to Pritchett. He could not afford to lose his cattle.

As Jay watched the sky brighten, he knew Pritchett's men would have already left town. There should be minimal resistance for Jay to deal with in Bronco. Afterward, with Pritchett dead, the proverbial head of the snake removed, the rest of the gunmen would have no leader and, therefore, no reason to continue harassing the farmers. Most would simply leave town, while the few that remained would be hunted down by lawmen arriving over the next few days.

Jay looked at the sky. He'd find out soon enough if the farmers—and his plan—were successful.

He turned his thoughts back to Marabelle. He was in love with her. He had no doubts about his feelings. Or about hers. But now, he'd discovered that his past had touched her family in the worst way.

How could I hope to be part of a family that I've brought tragedy to?

He gazed into the smoldering embers, then closed his eyes.

How could I marry a woman when I killed her brother years ago? How could her parents or her younger brother ever accept me, knowing I killed Sam?

There was really only one choice remaining for him. He didn't look forward to going back to the long, lonely days and nights of drifting, of always passing through from one unknown destination to the next. The thought of a future without Marabelle tore at his heart and twisted his gut. No more horse rides together holding hands. Just an endless trail of going nowhere.

He felt a shudder raise his hackles and send chill bumps scampering all over his body. Never one for negative thinking, he was appalled at the thoughts tumbling through his mind. In years past, such thoughts wouldn't have caused him a minute of agony. But now, when he had come so close to happiness, his whole world had come tumbling down on top of him.

Jay tossed the remains of his coffee into the fire. No point worrying about the future unless he got past today first.

Jay knew Pritchett would have a complex plan to deal with him when he arrived. The man had to know Jay would be equally careful and equally complex in his opposing plans. So why not do something simple or even careless? Jay stood up and kicked dirt on the fire, completely smothering it.

Pritchett was the kind of man who took immense pride in knowing how his opponent thought. Everything Jay knew about the man and his actions supported this conclusion. It was important for Pritchett to know that he could outthink or out-maneuver his enemies. In that realization, Jay knew Pritchett would not even give half a thought to the hope that Jay would do something stupid. Wouldn't even consider the insane.

Instantly, Jay knew exactly how he would get into town.

Pritchett sat at a table in the darkness of the kitchen house. He was sweating. He couldn't figure out where his plan had fallen apart. He had carefully considered every conceivable action the farmers might take and had a plan to take advantage of their every action. He had them on the defensive, running and hiding, waiting for him to strike the next blow. He thought he was making them sweat. But the farmers were not sweating. He was the one sweating. None of his men guarding the herd had checked in last night, so he'd sent four men out to check on them. None of those four had returned, which meant something was terribly wrong. They had organized and had done the one thing he had not anticipated.

The farmers should have been frantically protecting their farms and families. He hadn't thought it possible that they could have gone on the offensive. They weren't cowboys or range hands or gunmen. They were just farmers. Dirt throwers.

Now, Pritchett began to suspect he had completely underestimated them. They had struck where he was most vulnerable. While he was expecting them to react irrationally and attack out of desperation, which he was ready to handle, they had deviously snuck around behind him and stolen his cattle. That was the only explanation.

His first reaction was to send out men to hunt down the farmers and kill them, then get his cattle back. Then he realized that was exactly what they wanted him to do. If he did, his town would be virtually unprotected, and Jason Peares could ride in at noon unmolested as he had promised.

Pritchett smiled in the darkness. The outlaw mind of Jason Peares was the brilliance behind the farmers' new tactics. It had to be him. He knew that only a man with his cunning could try to outsmart him.

Pritchett reconsidered the farmers' strategy. His men had disappeared last night. Ordinarily, if he reacted the way they wanted him to respond, he would have sent his men out immediately, or at least at sunrise, to hunt down the farmers and begin the roundup. Jay would attempt to sneak into town when he was sure all his men had been sent away. That meant Jay was planning on arriving shortly after sunrise, not at noon. Maybe even before sunrise.

That would be dramatic of him, Pritchett mused. But he would only be coming if he thought Pritchett's men had been lured away. If he discovered otherwise, he wouldn't show. Instead, he would adapt quickly with another plan.

This would be a rare opportunity, Pritchett thought. He had to get Jay into town. He knew if he killed him, the farmers would crumble without his outlaw mind to keep them organized.

Pritchett walked over to the doorway and called to Chuck Peters, who waited on the boardwalk for his instructions. He told him to send all but a handful of men out of town until an hour after sunrise. They were to circle back and surround the town, ready to pounce when Jason Peares made his entrance.

Then Pritchett went back to his table. He felt intense satisfaction with his new strategy as he settled himself back in his chair to await the coming battle.

CHAPTER 16

T HE LATE SPRING HEAT WAVE was no good for anyone, and it was going to be another scorcher. As usual the men gathered in the saloon for their morning drinks. A liquid breakfast prepared the men for their new assignment: simply wait for Jason Peares to arrive shortly after sunrise. They had been offered an extra $500 in gold nuggets for the opportunity to kill the man.

There were five men lined up alongside the bar this morning. They downed their last drinks and filed out through the swinging double door. Outside, the dew was still damp on the boardwalk, and the sky was early morning dawn-blue, cloudless, and lighting up fast. The sun was just past the horizon, looking like a bright yellow ball at the end of Bronco's main street.

Except this morning there was a dark spot, a shadow in the middle of the bright yellow ball.

The youngest of the five pointed up the street into the sun ball. Four more pairs of eyes stared, squinting against the bright glare. All five men were dressed in dirty, ragged trail garb, all were unshaven, and all wore tied-down holsters. The shadow in the sun slowly moved closer until it materialized into a horse and rider. Five hands shaded five sets of eyes as the rider moved out of the sun and rode directly toward them.

All the men could see was the dark outline of a tall, thin rider and horse, but as the rider moved closer, they could see that he wore two extra guns tucked into the front of his pants, butts facing outward for the easy grab. He fingered a shotgun balanced carefully across his lap. The rider rode up and stopped about twenty feet short of the five curious men.

"It's him!" the youngest one whispered. Their pot of gold had come to them.

Something about the morning felt wrong. Rumors indicated that Jason Peares was coming for Pritchett at noon. But Slade knew Jay. He might be coming, and Slade had no idea when he might come, but he was certain it wouldn't be at noon as he was said to have promised.

Shortly before dawn, Slade simply went downstairs and knocked on the door to the room where Miss Evans was being held. He gave the proper code word after identifying himself. When Hank opened the door, Slade popped him hard on the side of the head with his gun butt. Quickly, he tied and gagged the man and stuffed him under the bed. Then, he led Miss Evans up to his room.

Slade sat on the edge of the washstand beside the only window in his room. From the second floor of the boardinghouse, he looked down on Bronco's main street. He watched Jay ride up the street and stop a short distance from the men in front of the saloon. As the men squinted and shaded their eyes, Slade smiled and nodded.

Very clever using the sun that way, he thought.

Slade glanced over at Miss Evans, who was sitting on the bed. She wasn't afraid of him. Instead, she acted like she'd expected him to rescue her. He had waited until the last moment, not wanting anyone to notice her missing and start a search. By a process of elimination, they would have eventually tried to search his room.

Now she smiled at him before he turned back to the window. She hadn't said much since he rescued her, only that she knew he wasn't Jay's enemy. He hadn't told her about the pouch of Pritchett's gold that he wore attached to his belt.

In his side vision, he saw her jump at the sound of gunfire from the street.

Jay stopped short of the men, his hat dipped low over his eyes. He lifted his head at the last moment, more for effect than for any practical reason. He saw surprise wash over the men's faces, then greed. Wordlessly, the five men moved out of each other's lines of fire, fingers twitching, eyes darting. The one in the middle started to raise his rifle. Jay knew he would have to kill that man first.

A door opened in the store next to the saloon, and a boy walked out onto the boardwalk tucking his shirt into his pants. He froze when he saw the confrontation, then turned and shouted into the store.

"Ma! Ma! He's back! He's back! I told you he was comin' back!"

"Who's back?"

Jay saw the boy's mother step into the doorway behind the boy. Terror struck her face, and she grabbed the boy by his suspenders and yanked him inside, slamming the door behind her.

The five men stood unmoving while Jay sat on his large black horse waiting. The man on the right moved his hand slightly toward his gun at the same time as the other man brought his rifle up. The other three saw the movement and went for their guns also, not wanting to be the last to shoot. They all were the last to shoot. Ten shots broke the early morning silence. Eight of them belonged to Jay's guns.

CHAPTER 17

PRITCHETT WIPED MORE SWEAT FROM his forehead after watching his men get shot down in the street. He watched Jay dismount and walk toward the saloon, glancing around casually as he reloaded his guns by feel.

It was unbelievable to Pritchett how five men couldn't put at least one bullet into a lone shooter at ten paces, no matter how fast the man's draw. Pritchett never believed in legends, but he was beginning to understand how Jason Peares had become one.

He watched Jay reappear from the saloon and walk across the street toward the kitchen house. As expected, Jay must have made the barkeep talk. The outlaw gunfighter was coming for him. Pritchett walked back to the rear of the dining room of the restaurant and sat at the special table that was part of his final trap.

At first, Jay headed for the front door of the kitchen house. Then, he changed direction in midstride and walked around to the back door. He kept an eye out for Pritchett's gunmen, but no one stepped forward to challenge him. No rifles or guns poked out of open doors or windows. The elder barkeep said all of Pritchett's men except the five he'd just killed had ridden out half an hour before sunrise. Still, Jay knew Pritchett wasn't one to be fooled so easily. He expected a trap.

Cautiously, Jay edged along the back wall of the kitchen house and eased the back door open. It squeaked on rusty hinges. If anyone was inside, he or they now knew he was coming in. The front dining room was separated from the back door by a large storage room without windows. It was too dark. He couldn't see in, but whoever was inside could easily see out. He'd be framed in the doorway for only a split second, but that was plenty long enough to get him killed. It was a chance he had to take, but still he hesitated. Bold entries were for heroes and fools.

A pang of fear crept up his spine. After a moment of considering his options, the fear of dying conquered his need to kill Pritchett, and he backed away from the door, letting it close slowly under its own hinged spring action.

He had taken barely half a dozen steps back toward the side of the kitchen house when suddenly, as the door bounced closed, part of the back wall exploded outward. Jay was knocked off his feet by the force of the blast, then sat for a minute catching his breath. He realized then that Pritchett wasn't helpless or defeated, even though his army of gunmen wasn't around to protect him.

Jay shook the thoughts from his mind and picked up his shotgun, then walked into the blasted out storeroom. He had expected an ambush, but nothing as clever and crafty as an explosive door. The explosion hadn't triggered when the door opened, but when it closed. Pritchett had rigged it to make sure Jay was inside the storage room. The effects of the blast confined to that small room surely would have been amplified enough to have killed him.

Jason added luck to his arsenal of weapons. Then he took a deep breath and stepped through the rubble of the storeroom, into the darkened eating room.

Jay pumped the shotgun reloader, then stepped forward, shotgun barrel first, fingers on the trigger, ready for the slightest movement. The room seemed empty, but Jay sensed a presence. He swung to cover Pritchett even as the man sucked in a breath to start speaking.

"I guess I underestimated you, Jason," Pritchett said. "You're smart, just like I figured when I hired you. Thanks to you, the Bronco Farming Cooperative has dealt me a stalemate."

"Stalemate? You're beaten. You can't defeat the Cooperative. They're too strong, and they're well organized now. They're not scared anymore." Jay paused. "They can take care of themselves. I'm here about Miss Evans."

"I'm sure we can still come to some agreement. I don't suppose you'd consider making a deal?"

Jay's eyes narrowed. The nerve of this man to think he was in a position to bargain. He was stalling, preparing some final trap. He had to be.

"No deals." Jay raised the shotgun. "Stand up and move toward the front door. You're going to jail. Now move."

"Wait, Jason. I have a proposal you might be interested in. If we can just talk this out."

Pritchett just stood there with his arms spread out like he was at a bargaining table, talking while Jay prodded the gun barrel toward the front door. He was stalling, taking a slow step forward. He looked at Jay again or rather, not at him, but through him. Or behind him.

Instinct! Move!

Jay ducked and started to turn, hearing at the same time a guttural grunt and whoosh of air as something heavy passed over his head. He glanced up to see the biggest axe he'd ever laid eyes on smash his hat into the thick pillar.

Jay rose and side-kicked, slamming his right boot into the stomach of the shadow, but it was like kicking a wall. The man didn't even budge. The shadow just yanked the huge axe from the wall and swung again. Jay raised the shotgun with both hands and blocked the blade, but the force of the shadow's swing slammed Jay into the wall hard enough to knock the wind out of him.

Dazed, Jay bounced off the wall and fell to one knee. He brought up the shotgun to shoot the shadow, but as he aimed he saw that the barrel was bent.

The shadow lunged again, and Jay saw only the barest hint of light flash off the plunging axe blade. In panic, he rolled to his left, kicking out at the same time. His boot caught the man in the ankles and knocked him farther off-balance. Then Jay ran to the front windows, stumbling over unseen tables and chairs, and yanked down a blanket that served as a blackout curtain.

Light bathed the room, and Jay could see Pritchett standing against the back wall. The huge attacking shadow jumped to his feet and stepped into the light. Bull charged, tossing the huge axe with one hand. The axe blade whistled past Jay's head as he dropped to the floor on his back. He pulled both guns from his belt and fired as fast as his hands could work his guns.

Bull lunged down at him and grabbed at him as he tried to roll away. He clamped a massive hand around Jay's throat, and suddenly Jay couldn't breathe. He dropped a gun and clawed at Bull's hand with his right while he slammed his remaining empty pistol against Bull's head repeatedly with his other hand. But the man's grip only grew tighter. Even with twelve bullets in his chest!

Colors appeared at the fringes of Jay's vision as he dropped his gun and clawed at Bull's arm with both hands. Tried to twist it loose. But he couldn't break Bull's grip. Jay finally reached for a gun in his holster and brought it up somewhere in the darkness that was closing in on him. He pulled the trigger again and again, the shots muffled against Bull's body, until he could only hear the click of the hammer on empty chambers.

Then suddenly, the pressure was gone, and he was finally gasping for breath. As he struggled to push Bull's dead weight off him, he heard scrambling sounds behind the counter where the money box was kept.

Pritchett!

Jay pulled himself free and scrambled over to the table next to the bar. He gripped the top of the table with his left hand, pulling himself up as he got his feet under him, then drew his last gun and swung it over to face Pritchett. He stared into both barrels of a shotgun.

He chuckled as he aimed at Pritchett's head. "Too bad yours isn't loaded."

Pritchett glanced down for a split second, but even as he realized he'd been tricked, he pulled both triggers. Jay swiped the shotgun aside and raked his own pistol across Pritchett's nose. He reached across the countertop and yanked the man over the top and onto the floor. He took a deep breath and hauled the man to his feet, then wordlessly pushed him out the front door. As they stepped onto the boardwalk, they both heard the voice.

"That's far enough."

Jay realized as he lowered his gun that his plan had failed. Pritchett had outmaneuvered him yet again. He looked up at fifteen gunmen all pointing their guns at him.

CHAPTER 18

"ONE HOUR AFTER SUNRISE, MR. Pritchett," Chuck Peters said. "Just like you said. Put your gun down, Jay."

As Jay holstered his gun, Pritchett rammed an elbow into his stomach. His breath exploded in a loud gasp and, not yet fully recovered from Bull's near stranglehold, his legs wobbled, unable to hold up his weight. Jay sank to his knees. Pritchett squatted down beside him.

"You actually thought you could outsmart me, didn't you?" Pritchett laughed. "I knew what your plan was all along. Now with you dead, the farmers are going to panic without a leader. Before they can regroup, I'm going to hunt down every last one of them. They'll wish they'd never crossed me."

Pritchett patted Jay on the shoulder. "And by the way, about Miss Evans." He leaned in close to Jay's ear. "I had her killed this morning." He laughed again. "She's dead."

Jay lunged at Pritchett, or tried to. Pritchett's fist caught him under his right ear, and he sprawled face first on the boardwalk. Pritchett stood and walked out into the street.

"Kill him."

"I wouldn't do that," a new voice proclaimed.

Jay recognized Hopkins' deep voice. There was a sudden cacophony of metallic sounds as dozens of guns, rifles, and shotguns were raised and readied. Jay raised his head and dragged himself to his knees to see the farmers glaring down from the rooftops at Pritchett's men. The gunmen wheeled their horses around trying to pick out targets, but they were clearly outnumbered.

"They won't shoot," shouted Pritchett, backing his way toward the saloon. "They're just farmers. They won't risk their women and children."

Jay studied the farmers. The women that Pritchett spoke of were up there, along with some of the older boys, all pointing rifles down into the street. Jay found his breath and pulled himself to his feet with the help of a hitching rail.

"Mr. Peters," he called out hoarsely. "They may have women and kids up there, but there's more than forty of them and only a little more than a dozen of you. And they have the high ground. You might get lucky and hit a couple of them, but they'll slaughter all of you. You don't have a chance."

Peters was the first to throw his gun down. The others reluctantly did the same. Hopkins ordered all the men to dismount and lay face down in the street as the farmers scampered down and tied them up. After a while, Marabelle walked over to him.

"How long have you all been up there?" he said.

"We just got here," she explained. "The stampede overran their camp, so there was no one to report back here what happened. So Pa decided we ought to come back here, figuring Pritchett's men didn't leave town. We captured four of his men heading out to their camp last night. The two men we sent ahead to scout the town heard them shouting orders as they were preparing to ride out. We knew they were coming back soon to trap you."

Jay started to speak, then froze as Miss Evans walked out of the saloon. He walked over to greet her with a gentle hug.

"I thought you were dead. Pritchett said—"

"Oh, no," she said, giving his hand a motherly pat. "I told you Slade is not your enemy. He snuck me away and kept me safe this morning. We went over to the saloon through the back door since Slade wasn't sure if he'd get shot by the farmers by mistake. He's waiting for you now. He let me go when Mr. Pritchett went in."

Jay squeezed her hand and walked over to the saloon. Inside, he saw Pritchett standing at the bar on the far side of Slade. Slade was setting two glasses on the bar. He poured whiskey into each.

The good stuff, Jay noted as he walked closer.

"Join me for one last drink, Jay?"

Jay nodded and looked past Slade to Pritchett. Then he looked back at Slade. The bright blue eyes were still friendly.

"What are your intentions?" Jay said calmly.

In answer, Slade flopped the small bag of gold on the bar. It landed with a solid clunk. Jay shook his head sadly.

"We don't have to do this, Slade. It isn't going to make a difference. The farmers have already won."

"It will make a difference. You're their strength. If I sneak out of here with Pritchett and if you're dead, the farmers won't stand a chance 'cause they know he'll be back."

"You have a good point." Jay reached for his glass and the two men tipped glasses in salute, then each downed his drink in one swallow. "Well, let me load up, and let's get this done with."

Jay checked his right gun, then shoved shells into his left gun. He stepped away from the bar and faced Slade. Then both men drew.

Marabelle hugged Miss Evans and was just reaching for her mother's embrace when the roar of gunshots broke through the cheering and celebration out in the street. Instant silence filled the air after the first two shots. Then three more quick shots rang out, then two more. A last, single shot finalized the event.

No one moved for a long time. Finally, slow, halting footsteps echoed on the wood floor of the saloon, and the double doors parted. Slade stepped out into the sunlight and paused. He looked around, then his gaze settled almost apologetically on Miss Evans. She stepped forward.

Marabelle's heart sank, and she covered her face. But the vision of Slade was etched into her memory. Three splotches of blood grew rapidly on his shirt. And he had walked out alive. Jay must be dead.

She took a deep breath and lowered her hands. She saw Miss Evans standing in front of Slade.

"I'm sorry, ma'am," he said quietly. He reached over to lean against the hitching post but missed and sprawled to his hands and knees in the street. Miss Evans knelt down beside him and cradled him as he fell over in her lap.

Marabelle walked slowly toward the saloon, pushed open the saloon double doors, and froze.

Jay stood at the bar awkwardly trying to pour himself a glass of whiskey with his left hand. His right arm was bloody, and he held it tightly against his side.

She approached slowly. As she watched, he grimaced in pain, his pouring hand unsteady and shaking. Then he coughed, his sudden movement causing him to overfill the tiny glass. He coughed again, and the bottle slipped out of his hands, spilling its contents over the bar. He sagged against the bar but made no effort to stand the bottle upright.

"Jay, are you all right?"

"No." He drank from the full glass of whiskey and nearly choked. "I got a bullet in my gut and one in my arm. And I just killed a man I respected."

"What happened?"

"He had one gun, I had two. I knew he'd aim for my right arm, my fast draw. So I drew with both guns. After that, I guess it was all about who could take the most lead and keep shooting."

"I'm so sorry. Here, let me help you." She moved to steady him.

"No, Marabelle," he said slowly. "You don't understand." He turned and looked at her. "Slade was someone I considered a friend, and I had to kill him, even after Miss Evans said he wasn't my enemy."

"But you didn't have any other choice."

"It was like this with Sam." He looked away.

Marabelle wrapped her arm around his shoulder and guided him out of the saloon. At the last moment, she noticed Pritchett's body lying on the floor near the bar. Jay saw her gaze and shrugged.

"I suppose he must've caught a stray shot."

Outside, they stopped beside Slade's body. Miss Evans had taken her shawl off and covered his head and shoulders. Jay and Marabelle walked over to the crowd of farmers.

"It's hard to celebrate," Mr. Boykin was saying. "We'll have to start over with practically nothing. We lost everything."

"The way I see it," Jay said. "You'll have to start by rounding up cattle that, by all accounts, now belongs to the Bronco Farming Cooperative. It'll take awhile."

He glanced around at surprised faces.

"Hell, we don't know anything about cattle," Mr. Boykin said.

"When you got here twenty years ago, I'll bet you didn't know much about farming either."

"You have a point, Jay," added Hopkins. "All we have to do is fatten 'em up and sell 'em to somebody."

The crowd took up the idea and began debating the possibilities of running the cattle to pay for rebuilding the farms. Jay and Marabelle walked over to his horse. Miss Evans and all of the Hopkins followed.

"Are you leaving?" Miss Evans asked.

"You said it's what I do best."

She nodded.

"Where are you going to go?" Marabelle had a defeated look on her face. He could tell she had already accepted the inevitable.

Jay looked over at Mr. Hopkins and Miss Clara. Neither spoke. Then, he looked over their shoulders toward the open land beyond the town. He could see the loneliness, the pain, the memories all waiting for him out there. Waiting to keep him company while he drifted and passed through.

"Where am I going?" he repeated. "To the doctor first, and

get these bullets cut out of my hide." He touched the side of Marabelle's face and smiled. "After that, I'm going to hit the trail and round up some cattle. That's what I really do best."

Marabelle sucked her breath, eyes wide. "What?"

Jay looked over at Miss Evans. "You knew all along, didn't you? You tried to tell me that night at your home. When you mentioned something huge and dark and deadly, I now understand you weren't speaking about the stampede. You were talking about Sam, weren't you?"

Miss Evans stepped forward and touched his uninjured arm. "I didn't know about Sam, I swear."

Jay just smiled. "You told me I would face a challenge far greater than any I have ever faced."

"I was speaking about Pritchett."

Jay shook his head and looked at Marabelle. "You were speaking about love. About staying with Marabelle."

He spoke gently to his beloved. "I know I killed your kin awhile back, and I'm truly sorry. Maybe we can work through this. Maybe we can't."

"It's not going to be easy, Jay."

"I know. But I'm not going to run away. I reckon you all may tell me to leave some day. For now, I'm going to stay and face this challenge. Because I love you."

Jay paused and looked at the crowd around him, finally settling his gaze on Mr. and Mrs. Hopkins. Then he smiled at Marabelle.

"We'll see what happens."

TO BE CONTINUED

If you enjoyed this adventure, check out the next book in the Jason Peares saga at JeffreyPostonBooks.com or wherever you buy books. Please let other readers know what you thought of the book by leaving a brief review at your favorite retailer. It only takes a moment and reviews are very valuable to authors.

ABOUT THE AUTHOR

Jeffrey Poston is the acclaimed author of the Jason Peares historical western series, as well as the fast-paced adventure thriller series *American Terrorist* and *Call Sign: Raven*. Blending traditional and revisionist historical research, his historical westerns have been praised as "fast-moving" (Kelton) and "exciting, page-turning" (Zollinger) and "among the best writers of westerns" (Biblio.com). His thriller books are lauded as "so realistic," "powerfully intense," and "action-packed page turners." He is a self-described *Rambling Man* and writes his novels wherever he happens to be in his travels.

Find Jeffrey at http://www.jeffreypostonbooks.com/

Amazon.com: http://amazon.com/author/jeffreyposton

Facebook: http://www.facebook.com/JeffreyPostonBooks

Twitter: http://www.twitter.com/BooksByJPoston

Goodreads: http://www.goodreads.com/JeffreyPoston

ACKNOWLEDGMENTS

As writers, we often go into our creative caves to compose a book, but when we come out, there are often dozens of people who help refine a story and turn it into a really good book. No writer can succeed without this special group of people—critical readers, cover artists, professional editors, marketing and PR specialists, and publishers.

I especially want to thank my critical reader and sounding board, Dr. Stephanie McIver. She's helped me through many of my books, offering insight and analysis that added depth and breadth to my characters and my plot.

Special thanks to Debra L. Hartmann, The Pro Book Editor, and her team for copyediting and proofreading. I also want to give a shout-out to the cover art designers of my books: Deanna Dionne.

I'm also thankful for the active imaginations (and the suspension of disbelief) of all the readers who enjoyed my Western and Thriller adventures. I'm especially grateful to the dozens of beta-readers who previewed the book and sent back invaluable advice. Your help means the world to this author!

www.ingramcontent.com/pod-product-compliance
Lightning Source LLC
Chambersburg PA
CBHW020526120726
47904CB00003B/973